THE FALLS OF LINGARRY

When her cousin Davina disappeared, Ailsa found herself involved. Had Davina, as her husband Iain suspected, run away with Alec McNair? Happily, Alec was not guilty, although he admitted to Ailsa that he would have married Davina had she not chosen Iain instead. Ailsa discovered how attractive Iain was — in spite of the friendship that was also growing between her and Alec. But how could any happiness come to Ailsa when, with both men, Davina would always come first?

Books by Mary Jane Warmington in the Linford Romance Library:

NURSE VICTORIA
WILD POPPY
THE STRANGERS AT BRIERY HALL
MISTRESS OF ELVAN HALL

MARY JANE WARMINGTON

THE FALLS OF LINGARRY

Complete and Unabridged

LINFORD
Leicester

First published in Great Britain
under the name of 'Mary Cummins'

First Linford Edition
published 2000

All the characters in this book have no
existence outside the imagination of the Author,
and have no relation whatsoever to anyone
bearing the same name or names. They are
not even distantly inspired by any individual
known or unknown to the Author, and all the
incidents are pure invention.

British Library CIP Data

Warmington, Mary Jane
    The falls of Lingarry.—Large print ed.—
Linford romance library
1. Love stories
2. Large type books
I. Title
823.9'14 [F]

ISBN 0–7089–5734–X

GLOUCESTERSHIRE

CLASS

COUNTY LIBRARY

Published by
F. A. Thorpe (Publishing)
Anstey, Leicestershire

Set by Words & Graphics Ltd.
Anstey, Leicestershire
Printed and bound in Great Britain by
T. J. International Ltd., Padstow, Cornwall

This book is printed on acid-free paper

1

Ailsa Kennedy drove through Fort William, having stopped her car in the outskirts to eat an excellent lunch. As she took the road for Inverness, then turned off towards Kyle of Lochalsh, the weather began to change and heavy clouds brought a sombre look to the mountains.

Ailsa shivered and turned on the car heater, even though it had been warm for May. She remembered this same journey which she had done just two months ago, when she had driven north to Kilcraig from her flat in Glasgow, to be bridesmaid to her cousin Davina. How things can change in two months, thought Ailsa sadly. How happy Davina had seemed, as a young bride, with handsome Iain McLaren for a bridegroom.

Yet now she had walked out on

her marriage, with, according to Aunt Elizabeth, no thought to spare for anybody but herself.

It had only been two days ago since she received her aunt's telephone call when she got back to her small flat one evening.

'Hello . . . Ailsa? Is that you, Ailsa?'

'Speaking. Hello, Aunt Elizabeth.'

It was easy to recognise her aunt's rather strident voice.

'Is Davina with you?' she asked, and Ailsa paused, hearing her aunt's voice trembling a little with uncertainty. 'She . . . she hasn't decided to come down to you to do some shopping, has she?'

'No, Aunt Elizabeth. At least . . . I've only just come in from the office. I can ask Mrs Davidson if anyone has called to see me . . . if you'd like to hold on . . . ?'

'Do that, dear.'

Ailsa put down the telephone and hurried across the landing to her nearest neighbour, but Mrs Davidson had heard no one at Ailsa's door. That meant, the girl decided, that no one *had* been there, or Mrs Davidson would have known!

'Hello, Aunt Elizabeth,' she said, again picking up the telephone. 'Sorry, but Davina hasn't been here. Maybe she's just decided to shop on her own.'

There was a long silence, and she heard her aunt's rather heavy breathing.

'Aunt Elizabeth?' she said tentatively. 'Maybe she'll call later when her shopping is finished. She knows she can always have a bed here for the night. Has she come by car, or by train?'

'Look, Ailsa!' Aunt Elizabeth's voice was husky. 'Can you come up to Kilcraig this weekend?'

'Well, I'd planned to go home. I'm due a week's holiday from the office, and I thought I'd take it this week.'

'I think you'd better come up here instead, Ailsa.' Elizabeth's voice grew hoarse. 'Your Uncle Robert's in America, and Hugh is in charge of

3

the office in Edinburgh. He . . . he'll come home as soon as he can. I . . . I was supposed to be going with Robert, but . . .'

Ailsa swallowed her astonishment, feeling an odd, nameless fear as she heard her aunt sob. She'd never heard Aunt Elizabeth cry in her life! Uncle Robert was chairman of a large firm selling and exporting fine tweeds, and her cousin, Hugh, was quite able to take charge of the company. When Ailsa had trained as a secretary, Hugh had wanted her to take a position with their company, but she had wanted independence, and had preferred to find a suitable post in Glasgow. Her parents and two young brothers lived in Ayr, and she found Glasgow rather more convenient than Edinburgh. Besides, Hugh and she had different ideas over marriage between cousins.

But now she was wishing that she had Hugh nearer at hand. She felt worried and frightened now that her aunt was so upset.

'Janet . . . your mother . . . won't mind if you come to Kilcraig instead of going home. I . . . I'll give her a ring.' Aunt Elizabeth's voice grew decisive, and much more like herself. 'Davina has . . . disappeared,' she said, with an effort. 'She's been gone four days now, Ailsa. I . . . I had hoped she'd have come down to you. I've tried to ring several times, but there was no reply.'

'I've been working late. Besides, Aunt Elizabeth, I'm not the only one she knows,' said Ailsa, hoping she sounded more cheerful than she felt.

'Doesn't Iain know where she is?'

There was another short silence.

'We can talk about it when you come, Ailsa,' Aunt Elizabeth said presently. 'Which day can you travel?'

'Friday,' said Ailsa, her mind busy with plans. 'I'll drive up. The Mini will be handy at Kilcraig.'

'Very well, dear. I'll get Bella Donaldson to prepare your room. Will your old one do or . . . or would you like Davina's?'

Again Ailsa swallowed her surprise. Davina's room was large and luxurious, and even after she married, Aunt Elizabeth had said she would keep it for Davina. Ailsa had always been put in a smaller back bedroom, which, oddly enough, she liked a great deal better.

'The bedroom I usually have will be fine,' she said reassuringly.

'Very well, dear. I'll see you on Friday.'

Ailsa had hung up, her brows wrinkled in thought. How could Davina have disappeared? And what about her husband, Iain McLaren of Cardalloch? Wouldn't he know where she had gone? They had only been married for two months, after all.

Nevertheless there must be something seriously wrong when Aunt Elizabeth would pass up a trip to America.

Ailsa kept to her arrangements with regard to her holiday, only she substituted Kilcraig for Ayr, and her aunt's large rambling old house set in the middle of a fair-sized estate in the Highlands for her parents' modest detached house on the outskirts of Ayr.

Ailsa's mother had been Janet Campbell, Elizabeth's only sister. She had been brought up in Kilcraig, but she had married James Kennedy, a gentle man of modest means, against her parents' wishes. It had made little difference to Janet that Elizabeth had inherited Kilcraig. She was the older sister and entitled to the property.

It was perhaps significant, however, thought Ailsa as she drove north, her mind on both her mother and her aunt, that when Elizabeth married Robert Dene, he had changed his name to include Campbell. So there were still Campbells living at Kilcraig.

Janet had been quite agreeable, if rather disappointed, about Ailsa's change of plans.

'Your Aunt Elizabeth seems to want you badly, darling,' she said on the telephone. 'She's just been speaking

7

to me on the phone, and it looks like Davina has just walked out. I expect she's had a tiff with her husband. She was always rather an indulged girl.'

'But not irresponsible, Mother,' defended Ailsa, who was very fond of her only girl cousin.

'Of course not, dear. You'd better go and see what it's all about. I'll try to pop up to Glasgow and see you after your holiday, or perhaps you could manage home for a weekend.'

'I'll try, Mother,' promised Ailsa. 'Love to Daddy and the boys.'

Her home was so different from Kilcraig, she thought, nostalgically, as she drove on, her eye caught by the grandeur of the Five Sisters of Kintail. Towards Dornie, she drove into a lay-by and paused to admire Eilean Donan Castle in its unique setting, thinking how the ancient castle had been so carefully restored. Uncle Robert had also been generous in restoring Kilcraig, and didn't hesitate to spend the wealth which came from his fine, successful business on the estate.

The cottages in the small village were well kept and modernised, though Ailsa had often noticed that it was Iain McLaren of Cardalloch who seemed to have the love and respect of the local people much more than Uncle Robert or Aunt Elizabeth. Perhaps that was why her aunt had been so proud to see Davina mistress of Cardalloch.

It had been a lovely wedding, thought Ailsa, as she drove further north, then took a narrow inland road between loch and mountain, where the going was slow because of having to back up to a passing place if she met another car. Finally the long, low white house came into view, part of it reflected in the still waters of the loch with the mountains towering behind like an enormous backcloth. To the left the narrow road turned off towards Cardalloch, and Ailsa paused, feeling tempted to drive on and see what Iain McLaren had to say about Davina, before she faced Aunt Elizabeth.

The moment passed, however, and she drove on through the wide white gates, her wheels crunching on the gravel. Almost before she stopped, Aunt Elizabeth was at the main door, hurrying out to welcome her, and Ailsa had to bite back an exclamation at the sight of her aunt. Elizabeth Campbell-Dene had aged ten years in two months.

At the wedding she had been a tall, imposing figure, her grey hair carefully cut and set, her clothing in perfect taste for the occasion. But now she wore a shapeless old cardigan and tweed skirt which were sadly in need of a press, and her hair looked straggly and had been pinned back haphazardly. Her keen black eyes were red-rimmed, and Ailsa could see the evidence of tears in her swollen lids.

'Oh, Ailsa,' she cried. 'Come in, dear. I'm so glad you're here.'

'So am I,' smiled Ailsa, feeling the fatigue of her journey as she walked round to the boot of her car to lift out her case.

'Let Hector do that,' protested Aunt Elizabeth. 'He and Bella will be in the kitchen likely. I . . . I've been watching for you from the window of the drawing room. You'll be needing your tea . . .'

'And a wash,' Ailsa told her.

'Come on upstairs, then. We can have tea together, then later . . . later I'll tell you about Davina.' Aunt Elizabeth's voice trembled again. 'I could imagine she might have a wee tiff with Iain, but . . . but I would have thought she'd come home to her own mother, Ailsa. I would have thought so, wouldn't you?'

* * *

Before going back to the drawing room to join Aunt Elizabeth, Ailsa looked into the kitchen to say hello to Bella and Hector, whom she had known all her life. She almost collided with Hector who was hurrying out to get her bags from the car, and to put it away in the old stables which were now used as a garage.

'Och, it's good to see you, Miss Ailsa,' he told her, his usually stern old face relaxing in a smile.

'It's nice to be back, Hector. Where's Bella?'

But already Bella was coming to welcome her in to a blazing fire and a seat on her favourite rocking chair.

'I can't stay, Bella,' said Ailsa, rather regretfully. She loved the old kitchen at Kilcraig where she had often helped Davina to mix the Christmas pudding or a cake for someone's birthday party with Bella watching carefully while they stirred. Many a time she had had to be dried off by the kitchen fire when she had fallen in the burn, and scones and pancakes had never tasted so good as when they were eaten straight from a hot girdle.

'What's this all about, Bella?' asked

Ailsa worriedly, and saw the dark blood rush into the old woman's cheeks.

'You'd best let the mistress tell you, Miss Ailsa,' Bella said. 'I never thought Miss Davina was the right wife for McLaren, anyway. She was softened wi' far too much protection. She was far too soft and impressionable. McLaren's a hard man. He's . . . och well, your aunt will tell you. Besides, you know McLaren.'

'Not so well,' protested Ailsa. 'He was a lot older than Davina and me, and he was always away at school and college when I came here on holiday. Aunt Elizabeth liked me to keep Davina company.'

'You've every right here, Miss Ailsa,' Bella told her stoutly. 'It's Miss Janet's home, too.'

There was a short, awkward silence then Ailsa got up, reluctantly, from swinging herself backwards and forwards on the old chair.

'I'd better go and see Aunt Elizabeth, then,' she told Bella, who was busy

13

cutting sandwiches and buttering potato scones.

'I'll bring in your teas directly,' Bella told her. 'I've made your favourite oatmeal biscuits.'

'You'll fatten me up, Bella, and that won't do,' laughed Ailsa, though her eyes sobered as she made her way along the broad polished wood corridors to the drawing room, which had a large window built out, to command a view of the broad straight gravel drive as far as the gate. Hector had obviously been busy in the garden, thought Ailsa, admiring the wealth of spring flowers as she walked up to the fire where her aunt was sitting so still and quiet, waiting for her.

'Bella's bringing tea now, Aunt Elizabeth. Do you want me to bring over the small table?'

'Please, dear.'

Ailsa prepared the small table and a moment later Bella appeared with the laden tray.

'See that the mistress eats up, Miss

14

Ailsa,' she said briskly. 'She's been picking like a sparrow this last day or two. That's no way to go on either, letting yourself go to skin and bone.'

'Stop fussing, Bella,' said Elizabeth, almost automatically. 'I'll eat when I'm hungry.'

'Then you should be hungry now.'

'I expect we're both hungry,' Ailsa told her, with a smile. 'Thank you for the tea, Bella.'

In fact she did coax her aunt to eat, and saw that she was beginning to look a little better after some good hot tea. Ailsa talked a great deal about her job in Glasgow and Elizabeth frowned a little.

'It's not work for you to do,' she said, as Ailsa had suspected she would. 'You know fine I wanted to pay for your course at university, but you'd have none of it . . . none of you!'

'I'm happy as I am,' protested Ailsa. 'Daddy has enough to do with the boys coming up. There was no point in my taking a degree because my present job is as good as I'd get even if I were an M.A. Some of my friends who did take a degree have had considerable difficulty in finding the right career afterwards.'

'I still say you should have had your chance,' her aunt said stubbornly. 'You weren't like Davina. She . . . she hasn't got your brains, but she . . . well, we knew she'd likely marry early.'

'And she did,' said Ailsa quickly. 'What's this all about, Aunt Elizabeth?' she asked again. 'Have she and Iain had a tiff?'

'All I know is he came here looking fair white and blazing about the eyes, and asked if Davina had come here. I don't know if they'd had a row. He refused to say and he's not the man you can ask. I . . . I don't know how their marriage went. She wouldn't tell me and I didn't ask, but I could see it wasn't plain sailing to begin with. Iain's stepmother and his wee sister and brother are still at Cardalloch, though, and maybe that was a mistake since

Davina didn't seem to settle. There's . . . there's talk, Ailsa . . . ' Aunt Elizabeth's voice became hesitant.

'What sort of talk?'

'That Alec McNair, who lives in a cottage on Cardalloch now . . . there's talk about him. He writes books about birds and animals, and gives shows on the television. Before she married, Davina . . . Davina kept hanging around his place, though she swore they were just friends and she was just interested in his work. McLaren was fair mad to have her, though. He hadn't seen her for a couple of years and didn't know she'd grown to look like . . . '

'Like the Fairy Queen herself,' said Ailsa softly, and saw the tears again in Aunt Elizabeth's eyes.

'McNair is missing from his cottage. He's just locked up and gone away. And . . . and some of Davina's clothes are missing in her new suitcase. Iain thinks . . . thinks they've gone away together. He believes . . . she fancied herself in love with the man, though I told him that was nonsense and she never saw anybody after she set eyes on him again. I'm sure of that. Davina *was* happy to wed Iain McLaren, wasn't she, Ailsa?'

Ailsa thought back to Davina's wedding day, trying to see it anew with this information her aunt was giving her. Davina had said nothing to her about Alec McNair and she would have expected her cousin to confide in her. If she had been in love with Alec, and not with Iain, it would have been more like Davina to have wanted Alec instead, and to have married him even if it was against her parents' wishes.

Yet Davina had seemed happy in her marriage, though perhaps more excited about the actual wedding than the thought of her new life to come. In many ways she had been far too immature.

'She seemed happy to me,' she said slowly, and Aunt Elizabeth's eyes cleared.

'And she said nothing to you about McNair?' she asked eagerly. 'Oh, Ailsa, it would be so shameful if she just walked off with another man on top of marrying McLaren. I . . . I know Davina's soft and . . . and impressionable. I'm her mother and she means the whole world to me, but if she's weak, it's my fault for bringing her up that way. Old Nanny Gregg used to warn me. But I don't think she'd be cruel enough just to go away without coming to see me, or giving me any hint . . . without coming to say goodbye . . . '

This time Ailsa did agree with her aunt. Davina had always been a 'mummy's girl'.

'Where is she?' asked Elizabeth. 'Where is she, Ailsa?'

'Iain has no idea at all?'

Elizabeth paused.

'I've a feeling he isn't telling me all he knows, but if he suspected where she was at all, then he'd be away after her.'

Ailsa was silent for a while, thinking.

'I'd better go over to Cardalloch and see Iain McLaren,' she decided. 'I'll go tomorrow, Aunt Elizabeth. Aunt Elizabeth!'

Her aunt roused herself, then shook her head rather slowly.

'Find out all you can, of course, Ailsa,' she said tiredly, 'but I can't help but face the truth. Davina . . . Davina has gone with Alec McNair. She always wanted things till she got them, then somehow they bored her. Maybe . . . maybe she got bored with Cardalloch. McNair would be offering her something new. She's been a bit . . . strange since her marriage anyway. Dear knows what'll happen now, for McLaren won't be having her back if it's McNair she's with. He's not that kind of man . . . not if she's gone off with another man. And if she comes here . . . '

Ailsa nodded, understanding. When Davina got tired of her new love, and decided to run home, then her mother would be there to take her in, and love her, no matter what she had done. But how difficult it would be for them all in such a small community, with Cardalloch so close to Kilcraig.

'Have you told Uncle Robert . . . and Hugh?' asked Ailsa.

'I've cabled Robert. I had to . . . he was expecting me to join him for a week or two in America, but I've told him not to worry. He knows Davina. Hugh thought she'd be away to see you and to give us all a fright, and especially McLaren. Do you think we should ask him to come home?'

Ailsa shook her head slowly.

'We'll give it a day or two till we see how things stand. I suppose you have been keeping it all as quiet as you can, but somebody's bound to have seen her . . . or Alec McNair. In a small place like Kilcraig, it's bound to come out soon as to which way she has gone. I mean, even if she'd gone by bus or train, she'd have to get into Kyle, and that means somebody's car . . . '

'Alec McNair has a car. Davina can drive now. It was one of the things she was fair mad to learn after she married. Before that she just enjoyed other people driving her about.'

Again Ailsa nodded, rather surprised. Her cousin was a dainty girl, and she had always been nervous about learning to drive.

Her eyes went again to her aunt who was looking deathly pale and tired, and she began to feel angry with Davina. Yet she loved her cousin in spite of the fact that sometimes they did not see eye to eye. Davina was always quick to jump to conclusions without checking the facts, and even as she remembered this, Ailsa's anger cooled. Wasn't she being guilty of that very thing which had often caused argument between them in the past? Wasn't she concluding that Davina had, indeed, run off with Alec McNair?

In fact . . . cold fear touched her heart . . . could it not be that her cousin had gone off wandering about the hills, and . . . ?

Ailsa bit her lip, alarm in her eyes, and almost asked her aunt if a search party had been sent out over the mountains. Then she remembered the packed case which was missing, and relief made her feel weak and trembly. But for that case, Aunt Elizabeth might have been pretty well distracted by now, not to mention Iain McLaren.

'Why don't you go up to bed now, Aunt Elizabeth?' she asked gently. 'I can take over for you here. I expect there's a lot to do with forms to fill up and accounts to be dealt with, but I've helped you before. I'll help you straighten things out while I'm here, and I'm sure we'll have news of Davina soon.'

Aunt Elizabeth rose a little unsteadily.

'I knew you'd help, Ailsa,' she said tiredly. 'You're a good child. Yes, I . . . I've let things slide. I let John and Agnes McLean go off on holiday just before this blew up. John's a fine game-keeper and sees to the running of the estate, and come the summer months, we'll likely be getting asked for fishing permits from summer visitors. A lot of the cottages are let, nowadays, for the summer months.'

'I know,' said Ailsa. 'I'll do the fishing permits if you like.'

'There won't be many yet, but John's often kept busy in the summer sorting out rows over where people ought to be fishing. I . . . I wish I'd never started giving permits.'

Ailsa was glad to see her aunt's mind on something else, even for a little while, as she went off to the kitchen to collect some hot milk, and to have a word with Bella.

'I'm putting her to bed early, Bella. She's very tired.'

'She hasn't had a wink o' sleep for the past few days . . . ever since Miss Davina went off.'

'Then maybe she'll sleep tonight,' said Ailsa, rather briskly. She would talk to Bella later, she decided. 'Hot milk and a warm bed will help.'

'There's a bottle in already,' she was told.

'Thank you, Bella. I'm having an early night myself, but we . . . perhaps we can talk in the morning. I'll take over from Aunt Elizabeth for a few days.'

This time Bella's face softened with relief.

'Oh, that's good, Miss Ailsa. We'll all be fair relieved, I can tell you.'

* * *

Next morning was Saturday, and Ailsa walked over the narrow hill path to the wooden bridge which spanned the river dividing Cardalloch from Kilcraig. It was a broad clear river, with good salmon and trout fishing, and fine sea trout where it flowed into the head of a narrow sea loch.

This morning the only fisherman on the Cardalloch side of the river was a sturdy boy of about nine, who reeled in his line and grinned up at Ailsa as

25

she crossed the rather rickety bridge.

She had no difficulty in recognising young Stuart Dervil, Iain's stepbrother. Five years ago, old John McLaren had married Lena Dervil, a widow with a small son and daughter. Iain had been in his early twenties at the time, and no one had ever been able to guess how he felt about the match. He had always shown his stepmother the greatest courtesy, and when his father died three years before, he had given her and his younger sister and brother his protection. But Ailsa knew that Iain had a great love for the sturdy young Stuart.

She paused on the bridge to lean over and look down at the boy, who had ventured into the shallow fast-running water in his wellington boots.

'Hello there, young Stuart! Are the fish rising today?'

'Och, devil a bite,' Stuart told her disgustedly. 'The water's far too low. Are you coming over to Cardalloch, Ailsa?'

She hid a smile. Young Stuart attended the village shool and he had the charmingly broad accent of the local children. There was a large hole in the front of his dark green jersey, and he looked as though he hadn't seen soap and water for a week.

'I'm coming over to see Iain,' she informed him. 'I hope he's in.'

'He's awa',' Stuart told her flatly.

'Oh.' Ailsa stood for a moment, nonplussed.

'My mother and Anice are in, though,' he told her helpfully, 'and Ina Blair is in today and she might gie ye a cup of tea, but she'll be the thrawn one about making it. Are . . . ?' Here Stuart hesitated for a moment. 'Are you here to look for Davina, Ailsa?'

She nodded, wanting to ask questions, but deciding that it might only worry young Stuart to know that people were upset over her cousin's disappearance. She would expect Iain to treat the matter sensibly in front of the child.

'You'll not be finding her,' he said, after a pause. 'If Iain can't find her, you can't. He's looked everywhere. You ask Anice.'

'Oh,' said Ailsa again.

Stuart was making no effort to pack up his fishing tackle in spite of the low water, so she decided to leave him to his sport, feeling in the pocket of her anorak for a bar of chocolate.

'Here, catch!' she said, and threw it over to him where he caught it with delight.

'Thanks, Ailsa,' he shouted, as she walked on. 'Don't bother about Davina. She's just a scary cat anyway. She's a fearty.'

Ailsa paused, frowning, and wondered if she should go back and question the boy. Maybe he knew quite a bit about Davina's whereabouts. The moment passed, however, and later she was to remember it with regret. But she always felt that her own small brothers were best left to grow up in their own good time, and the worries and responsibilities of adults were something for the future.

Now she walked on up the narrow brown road until she came to the wide gateposts of Cardalloch. Unlike Kilcraig, the gates had been removed long since, but the drive was trim and quite well kept. The old house was of brown stone, long and low with broad steps up to the front door.

Ailsa hesitated, wondering whether to go round to the kitchen door and make her presence known to Ina Blair who was 'in today'. Ina had lived in until her marriage to Jim Blair, who worked on the estate, which was mainly given over to sheep farming and forestry. Again, unlike Kilcraig, Cardalloch had to pay its own way, and there was more evidence of having to make ends meet than at Kilcraig. Yet there was a solid grandeur about Cardalloch, and a spirit of people working together with a purpose in their hearts and minds, which was lacking in the smaller place.

Ailsa had often felt this, and had sometimes resented the fact that her Aunt Elizabeth was inclined to be soft, and would foot the bill for extras in the cottages which were neither necessary nor improving, to Ailsa's eye. She had often felt that her aunt would have had more respect if she had said no occasionally.

But now she walked up to the large solid oak door which stood open, and walked on through to the inner glass door, after ringing the bell. After a second ring, the door was thrown open and for a moment Ailsa stared at the girl who confronted her.

Rumour had it that Lena McLaren's first husband, Daniel Dervil, had gypsy blood in him, and now, looking at his daughter, Ailsa felt she could well believe it. She had scarcely noticed Anice at the wedding, as the girl had been clad in a rather old-fashioned dun-coloured suit, with the socks and shoes of a child, her hair secured firmly in two black plaits.

But Ailsa now saw that sixteen-year-old Anice was clearly growing up, and for a moment she was startled by the girl's beauty. Anice was no longer a rather insignificant little schoolgirl. She was a remarkably beautiful young woman, wearing a scarlet skirt and white silk blouse which had surely belonged to Davina, her long shining black curls rippling down her back, and her black eyes sparkling in a small, perfectly modelled face.

A moment later, however, the lovely, rather bold face seemed to change, as Anice recognised her visitor, and she gave Ailsa a sweet, demure little smile of welcome.

'Hello, Ailsa. Come in, please. Do you want to see my mother? Iain is out, I'm afraid, and . . . and so's Davina, as I expect you've heard.'

'I have heard,' Ailsa told her, following her along the broad corridor so similar to Kilcraig, but so much darker with polished black wood, which looked, to Ailsa, in need of care.

'As a matter of fact, that's why I'm here, Anice.'

The girl nodded worriedly.

'I know. She's . . . well, she's worried us all, Ailsa.'

Ailsa could see that Anice meant it, and her heart went out to her.

'We'll find her, my dear, don't worry.'

'Mother's been upset,' said Anice, in a low voice.

'Well, I'll try not to upset her any more. Er . . . Stuart said Ina Blair might manage me a cup of tea under protest.'

Anice grinned. 'I'll ask her,' she offered, and as she opened the door, then swung away, Ailsa again caught the heady sweet perfume of her black hair, and something stirred in the back of her mind, making her pause for a moment and try to chase a memory. It eluded her, and she smiled, remembering her own 'in-between' years when the child in her sought to be a woman by drenching herself in perfume, then the woman became a child again when she found herself involved in a situation she couldn't handle.

But now Lena McLaren was rising to greet her, and again Ailsa was shocked by the appearance of another of the Cardalloch womenfolk. She had always thought that Lena, now in her forties, was a fine figure of a woman with the classical beauty and proud carriage which went so well with her height. But now she looked thin and pale, her face lined and her hair streaked with grey, and lying in wisps on her forehead.

'Hello, Ailsa,' she said, rather stonily.

'Hello, Mrs McLaren.'

Ailsa felt rather at a loss for words. Lena McLaren had never gone out of her way to make a fuss of her, but on the other hand, she had always treated Ailsa with warmth and friendliness. Now it seemed as though there was hostility in her voice.

'I'm . . . I'm sorry you aren't feeling very well,' she said uncertainly. 'Anice

33

has just been telling me. I . . . I expect it's been a worry that Davina has . . . has just walked out without saying where she was going.'

Lena sat down and nodded, as though pulling herself together.

'Has her mother sent for you? We thought . . . we hoped she might be with you until Mrs Campbell-Dene said she had telephoned. Iain has gone to make some new enquiries.' Her voice grew stronger for a moment. 'Now she's been gone so long without a word, he'd be best to let her go. That's what I say. It would be best left alone. She'll turn up . . . soon enough.'

The door had opened behind them, and Ailsa heard Anice give a small gasp as she carried in the tray, and for a moment their eyes met, and she was sure she saw fear in the child's eyes. But Anice was smiling as she laid the tray on the table.

'Goodness, I thought I was going to drop it,' she said breathlessly, and

Ailsa laughed, realising where the fear came from.

In spite of her efforts, however, to talk to the other two women, the atmosphere was rather strained, as all three drank hot black tea, tasting of peat, and Ailsa ate a piece of Ina Blair's oatcake.

'Did nobody see Davina go?' she asked.

'Nobody,' said Anice. 'At least, I *might* have seen her, but I'm not sure. I caught a . . . a sort of glimpse of somebody hurrying away, as you might say.'

Ailsa listened, then caught sight of Lena McLaren's white face, her eyes burning as they looked at Anice.

'Why didn't you stop her?' she was asking. 'All this trouble . . . '

'Och, how was I to know?' Anice asked airily, tossing her black mane of hair, then she, too, began to look worried. Again Ailsa felt touched. They must both have grown fond of Davina to be so obviously worried about her.

Or could it be that they didn't like Iain to be so worried? Were they both concerned for him.

'Iain will be . . . upset,' she said slowly, and Anice coloured deeply.

'If she's left him, he'll get over it,' she said. 'She was the wrong wife for him.'

'Anice!' Her mother's voice was sharp.

'Well, she was. She was such a softie. McLaren needed a better woman than Davina.'

'Remember who you are speaking to, and who you are speaking about.'

Lena McLaren's voice was suddenly tight with anger and Anice looked like a chastened child again.

'I . . . I'm sorry,' she mumbled. 'I forgot she's your cousin.'

Ailsa stood up. 'When will Iain be back?' she asked, picking up her cardigan. 'I feel I'd like to talk to him.'

'Of course,' said Lena. 'He's gone to Inverness, I understand. Someone said . . . ' She bit her lip, then continued flatly, 'It seems that Alec McNair has gone off to Inverness. I think Iain wants to question him as to whether or not he has seen Davina. They . . . knew one another.'

'I see,' said Ailsa. 'Well, I know he's busy. I'll come back in a day or two.'

'You'll be very welcome at Cardalloch,' said Lena McLaren politely.

Anice said nothing, but came to the door with Ailsa.

'Do you think she'll turn up?' she asked anxiously.

'Of course she will. No one stays hidden for long these days, wherever they are,' said Ailsa, more cheerfully than she felt.

Although Cardalloch had changed little over the years, each mistress accepting what had already been given, small things had been added, and Ailsa had been aware of pretty cushions and a lovely new soft Chinese rug, which could only have been chosen by Davina. Somehow these small touches had brought her cousin nearer to her than everything she had still left behind at Kilcraig.

What if Iain found Alec McNair, and Davina was with him? What then? Ailsa's mind shrugged away from the ugliness of divorce, yet she couldn't see the proud McLaren bringing home an errant wife and keeping her as the mistress of his house.

Ailsa felt cold in spite of the warm winds, as she walked back to Kilcraig. As she crossed the river, she looked around for Stuart, but there was no sign of the small boy. She felt disappointed. She liked the small sturdy boy, and she would have enjoyed talking to him, already missing her own younger brothers. Sometimes she declared that they deserved a good thump, but she loved them in spite of it all . . . as Iain McLaren loved Stuart.

2

Almost automatically Ailsa went round the back of the house and in the kitchen door when she returned to Kilcraig. It was nearly lunch time, which Bella referred to as dinner time, and the kitchen had the rich warm smell of good food being cooked on a solid fuel cooker.

Bella had been given a very modern electric cooker last time the kitchen had been decorated, but she had pleaded for her old cooker to remain as well.

'Suppose the new-fangled thing breaks down,' she said to Elizabeth. 'What then? Do I boil you an egg over an open fire?'

'It won't break down. Thousands . . . millions, maybe, are in use every day.'

Bella had fingered the dials and knobs. 'I'd need an L-plate on it,' she remarked, 'and to pass my test before I could gie you some decent food cooked on it.'

'Oh, all right, Bella,' Mrs Campbell-Dene conceded. 'Have it your own way.'

Now the new cooker shone with cleaning and polishing, and lack of use, while pans bubbled and hissed on the old cooker.

Ailsa lifted one or two pans and peered in.

'Come out, miss!' she was told sharply, and grinned when she remembered how often she had been told that very thing. She had burned herself once, and old Nanny Gregg, Davina's old nurse, had bandaged her finger while she and Bella had 'words'.

'Is Nanny Gregg dead now?' she asked suddenly.

'Mercy on us, what questions you ask! What made you think of her?'

'Just thinking about the old days when I came on holiday. And Davina. Nanny won't know where she is, will she? Unless she's dead?'

'Well, she's no deid. But she doesn't know where she is either. She lives in a wee cottage further up into the hills, but her lad, Will, still helps at the forestry. Hector saw him only yesterday and Nanny's no' as fit as she was. The mistress made her retire, and that was a bad thing.'

'I'm sure Aunt Elizabeth would do it for the best.'

'Of course she did. Mind you, Jeanie Gregg and I never always saw eye to eye, but she was fair lonely wi' nothing to do. Miss Davina had her down at the wedding, though, and she came wi' a new suit up to her knees in the new fashion, and a fancy hat. You never saw the like. And her will never see eighty again.'

Bella laughed with amusement and Ailsa tried to remember such an interesting guest at the wedding. It had been such a big affair, however, and her duties as bridesmaid so demanding, that she hadn't seen anyone in particular.

'I'd better go and see Aunt Elizabeth,' she said, after a moment. 'I was over at Cardalloch, but Iain is . . . away.'

Bella mashed up fluffy potatoes with what she called a 'beetle', her face red either with effort or emotion.

'He won't find her wi' McNair,' she said suddenly. 'Miss Davina gave her word and she'll keep it. She's a wee soft thing, but she's honest. But I know something . . . I know she wasn't happy at Cardalloch. Something . . . somebody was making her unhappy. If there was somewhere she could go and be quiet for a wee while, I'd say good luck to her. Give them all a fright, and maybe they would look after her a bit better, but . . . ' Bella turned, and Ailsa's breath caught when she saw the unaccustomed tears in Bella's eyes, too. 'Oh, Miss Ailsa, I'm feared. I told Hector and . . . and he's been looking . . . out on the hills. It's easy for anybody, even someone who knows the place like Miss Davina, to slip out and get lost in the hills. You don't think . . . ?'

Ailsa fought down her own fear at Bella's words, then remembered that Davina had never been one to go out walking, especially by herself. Her delicate body tired easily, and she hated to get her feet wet, an almost certainty in the marshy ground among the hills.

'No, I don't, Bella,' she said firmly. 'Besides, what would she be going over the hills for, with her suitcase? She'd never carry it further than quarter of a mile.'

Bella's distress vanished and her voice grew matter-of-fact with relief.

'Och, I'd forgotten about her case. I bet she's just having a wee holiday, then, in one of the hotels.'

'Of course she is,' agreed Ailsa. 'I'll go on into the dining room, Bella. Want me to carry anything?'

'No, you'll just put me off my stroke,' said Bella graciously.

Ailsa hid a smile, then left the

kitchen, quietly closing the door. Had Davina just gone off to be by herself for a while? If she had, then she would have expected her to come to Glasgow. What was wrong that Davina could not discuss, even with her? And why hadn't she let Iain and her mother know, even if she had withheld the address? It wasn't like Davina to cause worry when she knew how worried they would be, or allow Iain to think she had gone off with another man, if she hadn't . . .

Slowly Ailsa went into the dining-room, finding it empty, but the log fire was blazing up the chimney in spite of the warmer day. It was a cold room, and not Ailsa's favourite, though she admired the lovely well-polished furniture and beautiful rich carpet and curtains. Bella must have decided to keep it as cheerful as possible, no doubt still inducing Aunt Elizabeth to eat, and keep up her strength.

A moment later Elizabeth arrived, still looking pale and worn, but neatly clad and with her hair tidy.

'Oh, hello, Ailsa,' she greeted her niece. 'Did you go over to Cardalloch?'

Ailsa nodded. 'Iain is away, up in Inverness, I think. I'll see him when he gets back.'

'After McNair, I suppose,' said Elizabeth tiredly.

'She won't have gone with McNair,' said Ailsa quickly.

She had thought over Bella's words and saw the sense in them, and if Aunt Elizabeth had not been so upset, she would not have doubted Davina either.

Elizabeth looked at her searchingly, then her chin rose a little.

'I should never have doubted her,' she said quietly. 'I feel ashamed, Ailsa.'

'Keep an open mind till we hear from her,' advised Ailsa. 'As we will. I'm sure of it.'

★ ★ ★

Iain McLaren came back from Inverness two days later, and telephoned over to

Kilcraig. Elizabeth took the call and Ailsa, listening to one side of it, was aware that he had not found out very much at Inverness.

'We . . . we'll just have to wait, my dear,' Elizabeth said rather shakily. 'Wait for news. She's sure to phone or write soon. She's probably having a wee holiday to herself, Iain. Maybe even buying a few clothes.'

She paused and turned to Ailsa handing out the phone.

'He would like to speak to you, dear.'

Ailsa coloured a little when she heard the deep tones of Iain McLaren's voice.

'I believe you came to see me a couple of days ago?'

'Yes. I . . . er . . . I wanted to talk to you.'

'Then I shall be happy to see you again. Would you be free this afternoon if I walk over to see you? Or would you prefer to come here?'

'If you're busy . . . ' she began diffidently. 'Of course I can come over. My time is free.'

'You are on holiday?'

'I've arranged an extension. I . . . I thought it was necessary.'

'I see.' There was silence for a moment, then he spoke decisively. 'I should be grateful if you could come to Cardalloch, Ailsa, this afternoon. No . . . no, just a moment. Tomorrow would be better, I think. Tomorrow at three o'clock, if you think you could manage that.'

'Very well,' she said quietly. 'I'll come tomorrow.'

'Thank you. Goodbye.'

She put the phone down thoughtfully. She doubted if much could be gained from the visit, but she found herself looking forward to it just the same.

* * *

Iain McLaren was a tall, broadly-built man with thick dark hair which hung over a broad, high forehead. His eyebrows were straight and black above dark eyes, which gave him a rather glowering look, but he greeted Ailsa with a warm handshake.

She had, again, walked over the narrow road, but today there had been no sign of young Stuart and she remembered that he would now be down at the small village school being soundly taught by Miss Frazer, the highly competent schoolmistress. Later he would no doubt be sent away for further education, but in the meantime Iain was wisely allowing him to grow up fine and healthy near his own home.

Ina Blair had opened the door to Ailsa and had managed a smile of welcome, but there was no sign of either Lena McLaren or her daughter Anice.

'You'll take tea?' invited McLaren, and when Ailsa accepted, he nodded to Ina who withdrew rather noisily.

Ailsa sat down nervously. There was something forbidding about Iain

McLaren, and she could sense the deep worry and unhappiness in his dark eyes as they rested on her almost absently.

'I . . . I'm sorry,' she began, and had to clear her throat. 'I'm sorry, about Davina, I mean. That . . . that you and Aunt Elizabeth have had to be so worried about her. You've . . . no idea at all about what has happened?'

She coloured under his gaze, feeling it was a foolish question. If McLaren had any idea, he wouldn't be wasting time roaming round Inverness. Ailsa looked at his strong dark face, and wondered what had caused Davina to want to leave his protection. She did not agree with Bella that he was too hard a man for her soft little cousin. Davina needed someone who would be like a rock to her.

She was aware of the silence as her thoughts raced ahead, while McLaren decided that the fire needed another log, and a good blowing up with the bellows. Moments later Ina Blair returned with a tray containing a pot of tea and some rather indifferent scones and biscuits. Iain's brows met, but he said nothing and allowed Ailsa to pour.

'My stepmother is feeling unwell today,' he said, sitting down. 'I apologise that Cardalloch is rather . . . disorganised at the moment.'

'Oh. I'm sorry,' said Ailsa. 'Is there anything I can do?'

'You're very kind, but I feel that Anice is old enough to do her share. She fancies herself a grown woman nowadays.'

Ailsa smiled, but McLaren's face was still serious.

'I went to Inverness,' he said deliberately, 'because I heard that McNair had gone up there and I knew that Davina . . . my wife . . . and McNair had been good friends. I wanted to be sure he had gone . . . alone . . . and if he hadn't, then I wanted to know why Davina had gone with him, so shortly after our marriage, without explaining herself to

50

me. I found . . . ' McLaren paused, his eyes again dark with pain. 'I found that McNair had caught a plane for London. He has business there, I believe. I could find out nothing more. He went alone, but that doesn't mean to say that my wife could not have been with him. There were lady passengers on the plane, several travelling alone.'

'I see,' said Ailsa.

'Your . . . your Aunt Elizabeth is right to wonder what sort of marriage we had when her daughter has to flee from her husband.'

'There's no need to tell me,' began Ailsa quickly, distressed by the sudden glimpse of his deepest unhappiness.

'We will talk of it once, but not again. I know you and Davina were very close. At first we were happy. I'm *sure* of it. I'm sure she . . . cared for me, as I did for her. Then something happened, though what it was I don't know.'

He got up and kicked at a log, sending sparks out into the room.

'She grew quiet, and nervous . . . and afraid even of me. I didn't know what to say to her, or how to reach her. She took to going out alone, learning to drive with Jim Blair to teach her, though I know she was always nervous.'

'There's no car missing?'

'None. We keep few cars at Cardalloch.'

'And no one saw her drive away in any other car?'

Again he sighed deeply.

'McNair's? No one saw him go either, only Rob Johnstone at the Post Office knew he was going to Inverness. His wife looks after McNair whiles. He and Davina were friends before our marriage. She swore they were only friends and I . . . I believed her. He's an interesting man and she enjoyed listening to his conversation.'

Again he sat, glowering thoughtfully.

'If she were going off with him . . . to leave me . . . I'd have expected her to leave the McLaren ring behind. She knew its place in the family. It belonged to my great-grandmother, a fine ruby, but we had to make it smaller for Davina. It's . . . still with her. I would have expected her to give it back to me, and to tell me why . . . to be honest with me. There are also one or two little things, personal things, I'd have expected her to take, if she was staying away as long as she has done. I mean, with some things it looks as though she has only gone away for a little while, but with others, it would seem she's not coming back.'

He sighed deeply, and hunched his shoulders.

'I've been very worried, and we've combed everywhere looking, in case of accidents. There was nothing to find.'

'Your stepmother . . . Mrs McLaren . . . she knows nothing? Or Anice?'

Ailsa again felt this was a futile question, but she wondered if there was anything under the surface, which she failed to see. McLaren sat quietly for a moment, his face pale and grim.

'I've questioned both of them. Lena was only too happy to have a new

53

mistress in the house. She's bad at organising things, and Davina could manage Ina very well. In her own way, Davina could get things done, and done well. Anice is still a child, and it was something new to have another girl in the house. I think she took an interest in Davina's clothes and things. They were together a lot, and I was grateful to Davina for taking an interest in the child. I wanted Anice to go to another school, but she is poor at academic subjects, and she was upset by the idea, and made me promise not to send her away. There's plenty for her to do here until she . . . until she is older.'

'Or marries. She's very beautiful.'

'She's a child,' said McLaren, rather harshly.

There was a movement at the door, and it opened to admit Anice, her black eyes sparkling and a touch of colour in her cheeks. Ailsa wondered if she had been listening to their conversation.

'Iain . . . ' she began.

'I'm engaged with Miss Kennedy,' he told her coldly.

'Oh. I'm sorry.'

'I'm afraid I must be going,' said Ailsa, standing up. 'I'll try to remember if there's anyone . . . anyone at all who might know Davina's where-abouts. I'll let you know.'

'Maybe she doesn't want to be found. Have you thought of that?' asked Anice, her eyes meeting Iain's boldly.

His face grew dark.

'If your mother is still unwell, perhaps you could go and supervise Ina Blair's arrangements for dinner tonight,' he told her sharply. 'She needs a firm hand, Anice. I understood you to say you were capable of running this house quite easily.'

Anice threw Ailsa a sulky look.

'Oh, all right, Iain,' she agreed. 'I'll talk to Ina. She's impertinent to me sometimes.'

'I'm sure you can deal with her,' said Iain tiredly.

He accompanied Ailsa to the door

and she felt pity for him stirring in her heart. He was a proud man, and this new worry, in addition to giving him so much doubt and unhappiness, must be eating into the most vulnerable part of his being.

'I'll come again,' she said impulsively, 'to see how Mrs McLaren is keeping. I feel sure we're bound to hear from Davina soon. She won't keep her mother in suspense.'

She could have bitten the words back as soon as they were said, seeing how McLaren's face whitened.

'No,' he agreed dully. 'She won't keep her mother in suspense. Thank you for coming, Ailsa.'

'Goodbye,' she told him, and swung off towards the road.

* * *

Ailsa stayed quietly at Kilcraig over the next few days, keeping an eye on Aunt Elizabeth whose moods tended to vary between anxiety and hope that Davina was only being thoughtless. This usually brought on righteous anger, and Ailsa had to listen while Aunt Elizabeth complained bitterly.

Ailsa herself was feeling anxious as the days passed, and wondering what to do about her return to Glasgow, her extended leave now being up. She was sadly aware that Aunt Elizabeth was in no fit state to be left on her own, with just Bella and Hector Donaldson to lean on, loyal though they were. After some careful thought she rang up her cousin Hugh.

'Is there no news of Davina?' he asked, a trifle impatiently. 'What's she thinking about doing a stupid thing like that?'

'We don't know,' Ailsa said, rather sharply. 'The thing is, Aunt Elizabeth is getting very nervous sitting at home waiting for news. I don't know what to do about it.'

'Can't you stay with her? I'm doing my best to get home, but with Father being away, too, it's very difficult.

Anyway, you'll be far better at cheering her up than I am.'

Ailsa bit her lip. 'I'm concerned about my job, Hugh,' she said frankly. 'It's a good job and I don't want to lose it, but I can't expect them to do without me for too long.'

'You know fine there's a much better job available to you here,' Hugh told her. 'Surely you know me better than that I would offer it to you just because you're a relative. Dene's hasn't been built up on sentiment. Can't you talk it over with your firm, and if they'd rather get someone else now, then let it go. I'll make it well worth your while, Ailsa. Between you and me, I'm worried about that young sister of mine, too, and I'd be ten times more worried if you weren't at Kilcraig. Doesn't McLaren know where she is at all? Or why she went?'

'N . . . not really,' said Ailsa, reluctant to explain about Alec McNair.

'Have you gone to the police yet?'

Her heart leapt, then grew cold.

Somehow she hadn't thought of contacting the police.

'No,' she said slowly. 'Do . . . do you think we should, Hugh? Somehow we've all been keeping it as quiet as possible. Do you think she might have set out to go somewhere . . . and got ill or something? Knocked down, even? But you'd think her address would have been noticed and they'd have got in touch with Cardalloch. It's on a leather label tied to her case. I remember seeing it quite clearly.'

'I suppose you're right,' said Hugh. 'Just the same, I'll make some tactful enquiries, I think, Ailsa.'

'Oh yes, please do,' she said, relieved. That, at least, would set their minds at rest, regarding an accident or similar.

'The local police already know,' said Elizabeth, gliding softly into the room. 'Iain had everyone out looking for her in case she set off walking and fell . . . '

'Oh,' said Ailsa, startled. 'I . . . I'm only speaking to Hugh.'

'I know. I heard you from the drawing room. Do take his advice and stay, Ailsa. I'd be very grateful if you would. I need help. John McLean is due back tomorrow. Maybe you could see him, and set things running smoothly again.'

'Very well,' agreed Ailsa quietly, and finished off her conversation to Hugh, then put down the phone and turned again to her aunt. 'We'll do it together. It would do you good to have something to do.'

Elizabeth nodded. 'All right. We'll work together,' she agreed.

John McLean was a strong, middle-aged man who knew the estate like the back of his hand.

'It's mainly forms to fill up, and ordering of supplies that has to be kept running, Miss Ailsa,' he told her. 'I'll keep an eye on the work being done. We've got some timber merchants coming to collect trees and I can keep an eye on all that. I'm . . . er . . . sorry the mistress is having to be worried, but I've no doubt at all Miss Davina will turn up safe and sound any day now. She's like a snowdrop, with a very slender stem, but resilient, too. See if I'm not right. And don't listen to gossip about Mr McNair. He's as fine a gentleman as drew breath. He would cause anxiety to nobody, even for a lady as pretty as Miss Davina.'

Somehow the words comforted Ailsa more than any she had heard so far. Everyone had been wondering about whether or not Davina would go with Alec McNair, but nobody had looked on McNair's side of the question. John McLean seemed very sure that he would not do such a thing.

Reluctantly, however, Ailsa got in touch with her firm in Glasgow, and asked them to find a replacement, then she wrote to her parents in Ayr, telling them what she had done. They might not be too pleased, she knew, because they, too, liked her to be independent of Kilcraig. Janet had always found

Elizabeth rather demanding, as well as generous.

But now they were dependent on her, thought Ailsa, rather wryly. That was rather a different thing. Already she was establishing a routine for the smooth running of Kilcraig, and she felt that the Donaldsons appreciated her efforts.

'You should get out a wee while yourself, Miss Ailsa,' Bella advised her a day or two later. 'It's been two or three weeks since you came, but you've hardly put a foot over the doorstep, except to go to Cardalloch, and that won't be taking your mind off things.'

Ailsa conceded the wisdom of this remark. She was beginning to feel oppressed by the old house, even though she loved it, knowing that many generations of her forebears had lived and died here.

'Maybe you're right, Bella,' she agreed. 'I'll go for a walk after dinner. I'd been intending to go to

Cardalloch, anyway, to ask after Mrs McLaren . . . '

'She's no sae bad,' Bella informed her. 'She's just a kind of ailing body. The girl is seeing to things. You can go to them another day. Get some fresh air into your own lungs today.'

'Oh,' said Ailsa, slightly at a loss.

Bella wasn't a Highland woman, being from south of Glasgow, but she was very good at speaking her mind, and giving sound advice, and it was usually wise to heed what she had to say.

'All right, Bella. I'll go down the river path to the head of the loch. Will that do?'

'That'll do fine. I'll pack you a few wee sandwiches, and a flask of coffee, and just you see that you relax down for a wee while. It'll gather some strength to you.'

Ailsa laughed, and after dinner she changed into a swinging, heavily pleated tweed skirt and a Fair Isle jumper, pushing her feet into stout brogues.

She had looked more elegant in the past, she thought, surveying herself critically in the dressing table mirror, but in a place like Kilcraig, it was the comfort which mattered.

But Bella's eyes were approving as she watched the trim, neat figure walking down the drive. Miss Ailsa might not have Miss Davina's delicate fairylike beauty, but she was a bonny lass nevertheless, with her russet brown hair, fine hazel eyes, and warm apricot skin. There was a wholesome beauty about her which was very satisfying.

Ailsa found that she had thoughtlessly crossed the bridge towards Cardalloch, her mind so busy with her problems, before remembering that she was supposed to be out for a walk. She hesitated, wondering whether to retrace her steps, then decided that she could still take the same walk, only on the other side of the loch. If she came across Iain, or any of his men, she was sure they would not mind.

It was quiet along the loch path,

which occasionally veered off through the trees, and Ailsa breathed deeply of the pure fresh air, feeling the sun warming her face, and the fresh green of new growth all around her.

She came upon the cottage before she had quite realised it, seeing that the front of it faced the loch, while the back was near the main road. This must be Alec McNair's cottage, she thought, unable to stop her own curiosity and interest.

The path divided and she knew she ought to take the right fork, which veered round almost to the main road, but instead she walked on round, and stood looking up at the neatly-kept garden and well-painted walls. McNair obviously kept his property in good repair.

It was some minutes before she realised that there was a curl of smoke from one of the chimneys, and that she was being watched with just as much interest as she was watching the house. A very tall man, almost as broad as

Iain, with a pleasant rugged face and piercing blue eyes, was watching her from a sitting position near the loch. He wore old breeches and leggings, and the smell of his pipe smoke caused Ailsa to turn, startled, even as she became aware of the white spiral of smoke from the chimney.

'Mr . . . Mr McNair?' she stammered.

'Alexander McNair,' he agreed. 'You have the advantage of me, Miss . . . Miss . . . ?'

'Kennedy. Ailsa Kennedy. I . . . I'm Davina Campbell-Dene's cousin.'

'Ah yes. You mean, of course, young Mrs McLaren.'

Ailsa coloured. 'Of course. I'm sorry.'

'Then if I may offer you my hospitality, please come inside. I see you've brought your own food with you.'

His eyes surveyed her mischievously, and she felt tempted to refuse, then thought better of it. She felt rather surprised that he should be here, obviously so unconcerned, while the question of Davina's whereabouts was still unanswered.

'My cottage is still a trifle untidy,' he apologised. 'I've been in London for a few weeks and have only just returned . . .'

'I know,' she said crisply, and he raised his eyebrows. 'Have you seen anyone since your return?'

He shook his head, his eyes sobering. 'As I say, I got back barely an hour ago.'

'I see.'

Ailsa sat down in a comfortable leather armchair, vaguely aware that she liked the long low room into which he had conducted her. A log fire had been lit, no doubt to take the chill off the room, but the white walls, gay rugs and deep leather chairs were comfortable and relaxing.

'No doubt, then, I'll be the first of many to wonder what you've done with my cousin, Mr McNair,' she said, watching him intently.

His expression was even more mystified. 'In what way?'

'She went missing about the same time that you went to Inverness, and took a plane for London. There's been a . . . a suspicion that you and she . . . you might have helped her . . .'

Ailsa broke off as the warm rich colour flooded Alec McNair's cheeks and his blue eyes suddenly sparked with anger.

'If anyone accuses either me or . . . or young Mrs McLaren of such a thing, they're liable to receive a good poke, Miss . . . Miss Kennedy!'

Ailsa could well believe that he meant it, and she sighed with relief, even as she knew what his answer would be.

'I know,' she said quietly, 'but please let me tell you about it, Mr McNair. I'm glad to have been the first to meet you since your return, then I can tell you quietly and who knows, you may be able to throw some light on where Davina might have gone. We've all been distracted with worry.'

She began to tell him, quietly, all she knew about her cousin's disappearance, nodding when he indicated permission for him to smoke his pipe.

'So she's gone somewhere, but where, or for what reason, none of us know or guess.'

'Not even McLaren?' he asked quietly when she had finished. 'I should have thought a husband who wasn't long a bridegroom would have known why.'

'He doesn't. I believe him,' she finished firmly. 'You can't blame him for suspecting you, even if deep down he knows he's wrong. He's clutching at straws really.'

Again the hot angry colour was in his cheeks.

'Mrs. McLaren . . . Davina . . . often came to talk to me and to look at my research on birds and other wild life. I earn my living writing books and articles, filming, recording and sometimes painting the wild life of our country, some of which is getting sadly depleted. I think Mrs McLaren found it a peaceful interest and was good enough to believe that what I was doing was worth while. I . . . I'm very angry that McLaren . . . or anyone else . . . could doubt her friendship with me.'

Ailsa could well believe it. Sooner or later he and Iain McLaren would be 'having things out', and she hoped that no tempers would be raised while they were about it, or one or other of them would end up in the loch, if not both!

'And she gave you no hint as to where she might have gone? She's only taken a suitcase. Most of her clothes are still at Cardalloch, yet the time is going past, and I would have expected her to want more of her things.'

Ailsa went over all the old ground, as much to ponder the matter herself, as to inform Alec McNair. He listened carefully as he considered, then he shook his head.

'I've only ever heard her talk about

her cousin Ailsa. I thought, too, that she was happy in her marriage and had a great love for McLaren. For a time . . . '

He was silent while he knocked out his pipe, then his eyes pierced hers and she could see the honesty in them.

'For a time, before her wedding, I was envying McLaren a little, and I didn't go to the wedding, though that was for reasons of work rather than anything else. However, that is all in the past. I soon stopped regretting her marriage, and was happy for her. She is as lovely and delicate as the most graceful of my birds . . . '

Ailsa smiled and decided that that, from Alec McNair, was probably a great compliment to Davina. Now that she had time to look round, she saw that his room was full of evidence of his work . . . collections of birds' eggs, books, papers, tape recorders, binoculars and other equipment.

'Well, don't ever start likening me to one of your birds,' she said, rising, and saw that he was startled. The blue eyes were watching her keenly.

'Why not? Birds are very beautiful creatures,' he told her softly.

'I prefer to be less beautiful, and remain a woman.'

His gaze swept over her, and she coloured, feeling uncomfortable under his scrutiny.

'Ay, yes, a woman . . . but not less beautiful.' Her eyes glinted a little with mischief. 'If you talked to my cousin like that, perhaps I shall have second thoughts about you!'

His hand caught her wrist. 'As I said,' he told her softly, 'I shan't tolerate unjust accusations, Miss Kennedy.'

Ailsa could feel the steely grip of his fingers.

'I apologise,' she said, with a small smile. 'I was teasing. I . . . I'm sorry. I shouldn't have said that.'

'Please come again,' he told her politely, handing her the haversack. 'Next time I shall offer you tea. At the moment I'm . . . er . . . rather disorganised and not ready to entertain a guest properly. I was even about to try for a nice fish when you arrived. Besides, you have your own tea.'

'Would you like to share it with me?' she offered impulsively.

Again the blue eyes looked into hers, but before he could answer, there was a loud banging on the door, then it was pushed open and Iain McLaren stood framed in the doorway.

'I saw your smoke, McNair,' he said, then broke off to stare at Ailsa.

'I've just met Mr McNair,' she explained awkwardly. 'I . . . I think I'd better go now.'

'Come in, McLaren,' Alec McNair was inviting, as she slipped out, feeling that it was better to leave the two men to understand each other in their own way.

A cool breeze had blown up from the loch and she shivered a little, hoping neither of them would throw in the other. It was too cold this evening, now, for such heroics. Yet something deep in her was very glad that McNair had nothing to do with her cousin's disappearance. There was a rare quality of integrity about him which she admired very much in a man.

She looked around for a likely place to eat her sandwiches and drink the tea Bella had prepared, though it was later than she had expected. It would be a terrible crime for her to take it all back home with her again.

But although she was within sight of the woodland path, McLaren still hadn't returned when she repacked the bag, nor had there been a splash from the loch!

So they had kept their tempers, thought Ailsa with relief.

But it still did not solve the most important question of all. Where was her cousin Davina?

3

Ailsa and her Aunt Elizabeth were busy in the study next day when Bella knocked, carrying a tray with a steaming pot of coffee and a plate of biscuits.

'Hector has just seen the doctor's car going up to Cardalloch,' she informed them, without preamble. 'It'll be Mrs McLaren, likely, poor woman. Ailing again. She must be worse, though, when they have had to send for Dr Baird.'

'Oh dear!' Ailsa looked at her aunt guiltily. She had been meaning to go over again to Cardalloch and see if Lena McLaren felt any better, and how the young girl, Anice, was managing to cope.

'You'd better go over and find out,' Elizabeth nodded. 'I'll give you some honey for her. It's useful in many ways.'

Elizabeth looked better today. Yesterday evening Ailsa had told her about her meeting with Alec McNair, and it seemed to her that her aunt was enormously relieved that he had no connection with Davina. Was it more important, wondered Ailsa rather wryly, that McNair should know nothing about her cousin than that her whereabouts should be known? Then her own cheeks coloured. She remembered experiencing a feeling of relief herself, when she found out the same thing, and she had no wish to explore her own motives.

'She'll have gone to one of her school friends most likely,' Elizabeth said, with a small sigh of resignation, 'though which one goodness knows. I thought I knew them all, and I've tried every one I can remember.'

Ailsa nodded. She had tried the only friends she shared with Davina herself. She was glad, however, that Aunt Elizabeth was looking quite a lot better, and the backlog of paperwork was becoming well in hand.

After lunch she went over to Cardalloch, and was appalled by the increasing air of neglect, as Anice led her again into the drawing room. The girl herself looked much more cared-for than the old house. She was wearing a pretty white silk dress with a broad tan belt and tan shoes to match. It was a distinctive outfit, and Ailsa had seen it before.

'Isn't that one of Davina's dresses?' she asked casually, and watched the hot colour rush into the girl's cheeks, and her eyes grow sullen.

'She gave it to me,' she said defiantly. 'Davina gave me lots of things to wear. All my own stuff is far too young for me now.'

'She's very generous,' conceded Ailsa. 'You must miss her a lot, then.'

Anice made no answer.

'I understand that your mother is worse today, and that you've had to send for the doctor.'

Anice stared, then laughed loudly.

'She's in bed, but she's no worse. The gossips have made a mistake this time.'

It was Ailsa's turn to colour. The girl's tone had implied that she was one of them.

'I'm sorry,' she said stiffly. 'I only walked over with some honey for Mrs McLaren from my aunt. I hope she is well enough to be up soon, then.'

As she rose, Iain McLaren opened the door and walked in.

'Hello, Ailsa,' he said tiredly.

'I was just going,' she told him awkwardly. 'Hector Donaldson saw the doctor's car and we thought your . . . your stepmother was maybe not feeling so well, but Anice tells me we've made a mistake this time.' She grinned rather shame-facedly. 'Please wish her well nevertheless.'

Iain was staring at Anice with annoyance.

'The doctor came to see young Stuart,' he said heavily. 'He's had to have his hand stitched. He . . . he's been bitten by a wild cat.'

'A wild cat!'

'He went off to play with one of his friends who lives in a farm further up among the hills. They chased the wild cat out of one of the barns, but Stuart trapped it and it bit his hand. It's . . . a bad bite.'

'Oh, goodness, I am sorry,' said Ailsa.

But a great deal of her pity was for Iain McLaren himself. He was a big, strong man, but there was an air of dejection about him, as he sat down wearily, and looked round the uncared-for room. His wife had walked out, his stepmother was ailing, and now his young brother was the victim of an accident.

'Look, would you like me to come over for an hour or two each day, and help?' offered Ailsa. 'Aunt Elizabeth is feeling quite a lot better now.'

'I can cope,' said Anice, her eyes suddenly flashing. She ran to Iain's side and sat on the arm of his chair.

'There's no need to bother Ailsa, is there, Iain?' she asked. 'Ina and I are . . . are trying to catch up, that's all.'

Ailsa's eyes were on the girl, dressed so prettily in Davina's silk dress, but she saw that Iain, too, had the same thing in mind.

'You're only a child, Anice,' he told her rather wearily. 'You could do a great deal here if you tried, but you just don't try.'

'I'm not a child,' cried the girl, tears sparkling in her eyes. 'You won't see that. You just won't see. I . . . I'm a woman now.'

'Fine silks don't make you a woman.'

'I can change. I can easily change out of this dress and put on my slacks and jersey. I was going to, anyway, before helping Ina. This was just to look decent for . . . for a little while.'

Iain's eyes had softened, and Ailsa could see that he had affection for his young stepsister too.

'Go and change, then,' he suggested, 'and you can help Ailsa. My dear, I'd be very grateful if you could just come over for a little while. We can come to . . . to some arrangement . . . '

'Don't spoil it,' she said briskly. 'I'll go home and arrange things with Aunt Elizabeth. I'll come for two or three hours each afternoon till your stepmother is feeling better or . . . or Davina has come home.'

'Thank you,' said McLaren quietly, and the words were enough to convey all he felt. Ailsa felt something like tears catch her throat, as he gave her his slow smile, and suddenly wondered what Davina could be thinking about to walk out on such a man.

Her eyes turned to Anice who was watching her, and there was a flash of anger and hatred on the girl's face. Ailsa felt taken aback. Obviously somebody didn't want her at Cardalloch.

But why should Anice be trying so hard to convince Iain that she was now grown up, and trying to do it, so childishly, by putting on Davina's clothes? Was he threatening to send her off to school again? Ailsa didn't think so, but she felt vaguely uneasy about the girl, feeling that there were depths to her which she couldn't reach. Anice was going to be difficult to manage if she came to help at Cardalloch.

★ ★ ★

But it was to be the following afternoon before Ailsa went back to Cardalloch. When she arrived home, a Range-Rover was parked in the drive, and when she walked into the drawing room Alec McNair rose to greet her, and to hold out his hand.

She stared a little. This tall man with the thick reddish hair, dressed in fine tweeds, was very different from the Alec McNair she had met yesterday. Aunt Elizabeth was obviously on cordial terms with him, because she looked relaxed and composed, if a little pale.

'Mr McNair called to talk about Davina,' she explained to Ailsa. 'We've been discussing . . . many things.'

'Oh.'

His blue eyes were resting on her with amusement.

'You'd thought to see a black eye?'

She blushed, and laughed a little.

'McLaren and I are old friends. We were boys together, and he should have remembered that before suspecting me of helping his wife to leave him. The McNairs had a small place bordering Cardalloch and Kilcraig, but it has long since been merged into both estates, and the old house removed.'

'Oh, I'm sorry.' Her surprise must have shown on her face.

'Don't be,' he told her. 'As I say, it was all a long time ago, and it would have cost a fortune to put the estate right. I'd have had to spend my summers showing people round at half a crown a time, plus a wee guide book and postcards. Not for me, I'm afraid. The McNairs have no sense of family pride. At least, not that sort.'

'More's the pity,' put in Aunt Elizabeth, then turned to Ailsa. 'How is poor Mrs McLaren, then?'

'Just the same, I'm afraid. It was actually young Stuart who was the invalid. He got bitten by a wild cat.'

She told them both all about it, while Alec McNair shook his head over the boy.

'I've promised I'll go over and help for an hour or two each afternoon. Er . . . I hope you can spare me, Aunt Elizabeth.'

The older woman nodded her agreement.

'Of course, Ailsa. You must do what you think fit.'

She was aware of Alec's eyes on her piercingly, and there was thought behind them.

'Don't do too much for them,' he advised. 'Don't get too involved.'

'Involved?'

He turned away and smiled a little.

'Maybe that was a wrong choice of word. Forget it, Miss Kennedy. Look, could you make it tomorrow afternoon instead of this afternoon? I wanted you to come with me.'

'Where?'

'To Kyle, first of all, then over to Kyleakin on Skye.'

'Why?'

His eyes grew guarded and he glanced at Aunt Elizabeth.

'Does a man need a reason to invite out a pretty girl on such a fine clear day?'

Ailsa sensed there was more behind his bantering answer, and she accepted a trifle reluctantly.

'I'll have to phone Iain, though, and tell him I won't be over till tomorrow.'

She went off to telephone, and to change into a pretty navy and white suit which gave her a trim elegance. She felt she had to match up to Alec McNair.

★ ★ ★

When she returned to the drawing room, she could see his blue eyes sweeping over her approvingly, though her aunt scarcely noticed that she had changed.

'I shan't be late . . . I hope,' Ailsa said, bending to kiss her.

'That's all right, Ailsa. It will do you good to get out for a little while. I've been thinking it wasn't good for you to be in here so much.'

Ailsa loved Skye. It was often shrouded in mist, but today, as they drove along the main road towards Kyle of Lochalsh, it seemed just a step away, across the narrow strip of water.

'I think it's just about the most beautiful place in all the world,' she said to Alec, as he drove the Range-Rover easily. 'Don't you think it's beautiful, Alec?'

'Yes, Ailsa.'

She coloured furiously, realising she had used his Christian name, and he grinned, showing white even teeth.

'We're old friends,' he told her gently. 'I've heard plenty about Ailsa from Davina McLaren, and I bet you'll have heard about me. Anyway, we've no time to be formal, if Davina is going to be found. I like both Iain McLaren and Elizabeth Campbell-Dene. Sometimes she has annoyed me in the past, but on the whole she's a fine woman, works hard, and does her best. Her only fault was trying to fight Davina's battles for her. The child knew this, and wanted to become independent. I think, maybe, she's doing that now.'

'You think you know where she is?' asked Ailsa eagerly. 'Oh, Alec! Is that why we're going to Kyleakin?'

'I . . . don't know,' he told her cagily. 'Only there's a small hotel in Kyleakin which Davina used to like very much. Sometimes I have to come over on business, and I've brought her once or twice before her marriage, and we had tea at the hotel. Today I want to do that again, only I've got Ailsa with me instead.'

Ailsa was listening thoughtfully.

'Why would she want to be

independent of Iain?' she asked wonderingly.

'I don't know that either,' said Alec, rather shortly.

They had reached Kyle, and he paused while they swung into the car park near the ferry.

'We won't take the car. It's a fine day, so we can walk.'

Suddenly he looked at her, and she could not doubt his sincerity.

'It's only a hunch, Ailsa, but I feel it's worth while acting on it. Don't be disappointed, my dear, if it comes to nothing. That's why . . . ' he paused, his eyes suddenly bleak, 'I couldn't say anything to your aunt. It's best that her hopes should not be raised too often.'

Ailsa nodded her agreement, and they went to stand in the sunshine and watch the small ferry coming in to dock, then they boarded her after the few cars and passengers had disembarked.

'It's quiet today,' said Alec, 'but give it another month and the tourists will be here in their crowds.'

'Don't you like tourists?' asked Ailsa, laughing.

'No objection to them at all. In fact, I like to see a lot of people enjoying the places I love. That's why I enjoy my work, I suppose. It takes time and patience, something not everyone possesses, and people in towns can only enjoy the wild life of our country second hand, as it were. It takes people like me to make a study of it, and share my findings with them.'

Ailsa nodded, her eyes on the vivid expressions on his rugged face. She had watched his wild life programmes on television herself, and had enjoyed them thoroughly.

'I'm mainly writing at the moment,' he told her. 'My last series of programmes has now been completed, but I've got quite a lot of writing and illustrating to do for a new book.'

'I'd love to see the illustrations,' she told him.

'Yes, all right. Those do take a time,' he admitted.

They stood leaning over the rail on the ferry looking into the wonderfully bright green of the sea, the seabed as clear as crystal. Shoals of small fish darted in and out, exploring the occasional empty tin which had been carelessly thrown into the sea. Then the ferry cast off, and they were away on the short journey across to Kyleakin. Ailsa breathed deeply of the fresh sea air, her eyes satisfied by the wonderful view of coastline, both on the mainland and on Skye. All too soon they were stepping off the ferry at Kyleakin, and walking up towards the tiny town.

Ailsa opted to look round the shops while Alec attended to business, deciding to buy herself a soft mohair scarf and one for Aunt Elizabeth. She looked longingly at some fine lambswool sweaters and matching skirt lengths, then decided to postpone buying anything else until a later date.

When Alec came back to join her, Ailsa asked him if they could take her favourite walk along the pebbly shore to the headland before going for tea. Somehow she felt reluctant to go to the hotel Alec mentioned, strangely afraid of the disappointment which she knew would lie ahead if Alec's hunch came to nothing.

'I love looking across at the lighthouse on a clear day,' she told him. 'I think it's one of the loveliest views I know.'

'All right,' he agreed.

They made their way to some flat rocks, where Ailsa spread out a lightweight mac, and they sat and watched the gulls overhead, and an elderly man wearing a thick woollen jersey, rowing his dog over to one of the islands.

'How peaceful it is,' said Ailsa, looking round rather sadly. 'One forgets all the horror and strife in the world, and all the human misery caused by human failings. Is that a good thing, Alec? Or is it like running away from one's responsibilities?'

'Only if we stay here all day,' he told

her, and she saw how the corner of his mouth quirked up when he smiled.

'It makes me sad to think of poor and lonely people who could be refreshed by such a view, but are never likely to see it. Sometimes I feel . . . well, guilty that I have so much, and others so little.'

'So much, Ailsa?'

'Not in material things,' she laughed, 'but I mean the love of my family, and good health, and freedom. In fact, the only thing I have to worry about is . . . is Davina.'

She was suddenly chilled and shivered a little.

Alec was gazing at her intently.

'Come on then, Ailsa. Let's go see if she's where I think she might be.'

But Alec drew a blank at the pretty hotel near the town, and although they ordered tea and sat down to enjoy some dainty sandwiches and cakes, Ailsa found she had little appetite for what she ate.

'Alec, I'm worried,' she said, after a while. 'Don't you think the police ought to do something now?'

'What has McLaren done?'

'He got the local police to help with a search and Hugh . . . you know Hugh? . . . he's also contacting the police. I expect it's to see if she is in hospital somewhere with loss of memory, or something like that. Alec, Iain says she grew worried about something, though she was awfully happy after their marriage, and I believe that. I can't understand her running away from Iain himself. You . . . you don't know what else she could have worried about?'

'Should I?' he asked, the cool look coming back into his eyes.

She felt rebuffed and drew back a little, and he moved uncomfortably, then apologised.

'You all keep wondering if there was anything between us,' he said, with exasperation. 'Well, there wasn't. Not after she married Iain McLaren.'

'And before then?' She couldn't help being curious.

'Before then . . . ' He broke off, his eyes brooding. 'Och, it's no use talking. But just remember that Davina is a grown woman.'

And he had loved her, thought Ailsa, as they walked back to the ferry in silence. Only she had married Iain. Had she, later, had regrets? Had her apparent happiness in her marriage just been a cover for something else? How Ailsa wished she knew!

★ ★ ★

Ailsa walked over the now familiar road to Cardalloch the following day. The weather had clouded a little from the lovely bright sunshine of the day before, and the hills, reflected in the loch, looked sombre and forbidding.

Her thoughts were still with Alec McNair, who had driven her home, rather silently, from Kyle after they again crossed on the ferry. Ailsa had invited him in, saying he would be most welcome to stay for dinner, but he had refused courteously.

'I'm afraid I have work to do this evening,' he told her. 'Thank you for coming with me. I'm sorry my hunch didn't come off.'

She nodded, her own disappointment lying coldly on her heart.

'I'm glad we didn't raise Aunt Elizabeth's hopes,' she told him wryly. 'Goodnight, then, Alec.'

'Goodnight.'

He drove away without asking if he might see her again, and she had gone in home, feeling restless and dissatisfied. It had been a rather depressing evening, and she felt tired now, as she went over to Cardalloch to see what she could do to help.

Anice greeted her, half sulkily and half with relief. Ina Blair had complained most of the morning, being bad at working without direction. She had no wish to take the blame for the gradual disorganisation of the house.

Ailsa, first of all, went up to see Lena McLaren who was lying in bed, looking very pale, with dark shadows under her eyes.

'What does Dr Baird say?' Ailsa asked, tidying up her bed, and making her more comfortable.

'I'm run down. I've got iron tablets to take, and I have got to rest for a day or two. He says I . . . I'm rather nervous. It's good of you to come, Ailsa.'

'I'm glad to help in any way I can. I expect you're sorry Davina has gone away like this.'

'Yes.' Lena's voice was barely a whisper. 'It would make all the difference in the world if . . . if she would come home.'

Ailsa saw that Lena was not looking at her, but beyond her to Anice who was leaning against the door, looking into the bedroom, her face still sulky.

'Perhaps if you bring some warm water and soap, your mother could refresh herself with a wash,' Ailsa suggested pleasantly, and looked Anice straight in the eye.

'Okay,' the girl said, and sauntered off.

Ailsa watched her go thoughtfully. She was going to have to deal with Anice one of these days.

Her visit to the kitchen was also received with sulky silence, while Ina Blair looked at her broodingly. She was a silent, moody woman, whose thoughts were hard to guess, but Ailsa drew a deep breath and explained her presence to Ina in a brisk and businesslike fashion.

'I'm sure it won't be long before young Mrs McLaren will be home again, Ina,' she ended, 'and it would be a pity to welcome her with a shabby house.'

Ina sniffed sceptically, and there was a sudden veiled look in her eyes. It occurred to Ailsa that she might be quite a source of information about Davina, but she would have to question Ina carefully. In fact, it might be as well to let Ina tell her anything she knew, or suspected, in her own good time.

Quickly she made a list of outstanding tasks, and borrowed one of Ina's own large flowered aprons.

'We'll make a start on these jobs together, Ina,' she said practically, and listed what each of them would do.

'All right, Miss Ailsa,' the woman said, then gave her a grudging smile. 'I'll be pleased to see the place running right again. The young mistress liked things nice.'

'Liked? Still likes, I hope.'

'Aye, maybe.'

Ailsa looked after her thoughtfully as she stalked off to scrub out the pantry, and she picked up her own polish and dusters. She hesitated, wondering whether she ought to go after Ina and ask her exactly what she meant, then it occurred to her that it was only Ina's manner of speech. Davina had 'liked things nice' while she was living here. Briskly she went off to brighten up the drawing room, plumping up cushions, and tidying up old newpapers and magazines.

The door opened quietly, and a pale-faced Stuart looked in, his hand well bandaged.

'Hello, Ailsa,' he said. 'Are you going to be our maid now?'

'Hardly,' she laughed. 'I'm only helping out till Davina comes back. How's the hand?'

'No' bad,' he informed her airily. 'I could have hunted that beast for sure, me and Davey, only I tripped over a coil of old rope and it turned on me.'

Ailsa eyed him thoughtfully.

'Weren't you afraid of it, Stuart? Wild cats are as fierce as they come.'

'Och no,' he told her scornfully. 'Some folk are far too soft, though that's mainly girls.'

'Anice?'

'No,' he told her proudly. 'Anice can do anything I can do. She can shoot and fish and climb. Can you climb? Have you ever climbed up to the Falls of Lingarry? I dared Davina, but she wouldn't do it. She said she'd only tried once in her life, and she wouldn't do it again. She was feart.'

'I'll go with you, Stuart, though I can understand Davina being frightened. It's a dangerous climb. But I'll do better than that for you. As soon as you feel better, we'll drive up past Killilan to the Falls of Glomach, the highest Falls in Britain, and we can walk from the parking place. That's a good tramp over the hills.'

Stuart showed a mixture of disappointment and respect.

'Have you been before?' he asked her.

'Sure I have.'

'But not Davina?'

'I told you. She's not a strong girl, though she has been up a little of the way with me, then she waited when it got too rough for me to come back.'

'She was feart.'

'No, she wasn't. She was just sensible. It's sensible not to do things if you aren't fit for them. It just means a lot of work and worry for somebody if you get stuck doing it.'

Stuart digested this.

'But she could do things when Anice . . .'

'Stuart!'

He looked round guiltily as Anice came into the room, her black eyes snapping angrily.

'Mother wants you.'

'What for?'

'Never mind what for. Just go.'

Anice spoke sharply, and he got up reluctantly. 'Okay.' He turned to Ailsa. 'When my hand is better?'

'When your hand is better,' she assured him.

'He spins tales,' said Anice, after Stuart had gone out. 'What did he tell you?'

Ailsa looked at her, surprised. There was a note of fear in the girl's voice.

'What should he have told me?' she asked deliberately.

'Nothing.' Anice was suddenly airy again.

'Is there something you know that

you are keeping to yourself?' pursued Ailsa.

'Of course not. If I knew where Davina was, don't you think I'd get her back?'

Anice turned and ran out of the room, leaving Ailsa feeling strangely disturbed. What had the relationship been between Davina and her sister-in-law? she wondered. Davina had obviously been good to her, giving her pretty clothes. But Stuart had found her too soft for his daring ways. Was that why Davina had learned to drive . . . to show that she was not quite as soft as all that? Ailsa sighed and looked round the drawing room. It was rather tidier, but much was still to be done in the house before it looked cared-for again.

'I'll come again tomorrow,' she informed Lena before she left. 'I'll have to establish some sort of routine for Anice and Ina. I'm glad you are feeling better, too.'

Lena was looking better with more

colour in her cheeks.

'Thank you, Ailsa,' she said gratefully.

★ ★ ★

Next day she found Iain still at home,
but ready to drive up the rough road
in his estate car to where men were
working on the forestry. He paused for
a word with her.

'I meant to get back early yesterday
evening to thank you, but I was delayed.
Cardalloch House looked very much
better when I got home.'

She smiled, her eyes crinkling, wishing
she could say the same for McLaren
himself. He now looked more in need
of care than the house. His jacket was
baggy, with a button hanging off, and
his linen was clean, but obviously had
not been ironed.

'Who does the laundry?' she asked,
frowning.

'Ina, probably. I don't know.'

He glanced at his own shirt, the

ready colour in his face.

'I washed this myself,' he told her coldly. 'It's perfectly clean.'

She felt pity for him, so she found it hard to speak.

'May I have your permission to supervise your wardrobe, and put it in order?' she asked quietly, and he hesitated for a long moment.

'I'm a relative, you know,' she reminded him, and he looked down at her, a muscle twitching in his jaw.

'You have my permission,' he told her, equally quietly, then strode off towards his estate car. She watched him go, the queer ache in her heart again, fighting down a sudden envy of Davina. It must surely have been worthwhile to have won the love of McLaren.

She turned to see Anice Dervil also staring down at Iain, as he opened the car door, and the light shining vividly on the girl's face made her seem far older than her years.

'She's right,' thought Ailsa. 'She's no

longer a child. She's a woman.'

Was Anice finding the old house restrictive? wondered Ailsa, as she turned again. Perhaps the girl needed young people of her own age to keep her company, and she had a sudden glimpse into how lonely it must be for her.

Again she glanced up, feeling that she must make an effort to be friends with the girl, and saw the hostile look back on her face. Anice certainly did not want her here, no doubt afraid of again being put to menial tasks.

But however much they were disliked, they had to be done, thought Ailsa, squaring her shoulders. There was far too much for Ina Blair to manage, even with the help of two women from the village.

As she opened the front door, her eye was caught by the dingy look of the broad hall, and she resolved to do something about that straight away. It was high time someone polished it up again.

4

For Ailsa the days began to pass erratically, sometimes grinding slowly, and sometimes at high speed, as she supervised the smooth running of both Cardalloch and Kilcraig.

There was an uneasy peace, however, in both households as Ailsa could sense the deep disquiet of both Iain McLaren and her aunt Elizabeth. Her cousin Hugh had paid a flying visit home, satisfied himself that all was well as far as possible, then hurried back to business again, after settling several outstanding matters with Ailsa.

'I'm feeling very worried now,' she confided to Hugh, 'though I try not to allow Aunt Elizabeth to see that . . . or Iain either, for that matter. I think they believe that Davina has just run away, but I can't help feeling uneasy, Hugh, in case she has met with an accident of some sort. Did . . . did you do anything about the police? I know Iain got the local police here to help organise a search, but it came to nothing.'

'There's been nothing from my end either,' Hugh informed her. 'Look, Ailsa, I'm inclined to think as Mother and Iain do. For some reason Davina has hopped it, and I bet it's something to do with McLaren.'

'Then why didn't she come home to her mother? She was always a mother's girl.'

Hugh's smile was rather cynical.

'Don't you think Mother would have encouraged her to go back to Cardalloch? Mother loves Davina, and has petted her all her life, but she thinks she made a woman of her, when I doubt if Davina has really grown up yet. Mother's old-fashioned and believes that when a girl marries, she sticks to her husband, for better or for worse.'

'And you call that old-fashioned!'

'Well, you know what I mean,' said Hugh impatiently. 'Mother certainly wouldn't shelter Davina for ever at Kilcraig, when she ought to be washing her husband's shirts at Cardalloch, if you see what I mean. And Davina is shrewd enough to know that.'

'Yes, I do see what you mean,' agreed Ailsa thoughtfully, 'and if she had come to me, Aunt Elizabeth would undoubtedly have found out. But oh, Hugh, if she'd even written a letter to let us know she's all right, what a difference it would have made. She need not have put an address.'

'I know.' This time Hugh's face was rather grim. 'I'll have something to say to my little sister when we do find her again!'

'I think we'll all be so pleased to see her, we'll only welcome her with love,' Ailsa said longingly. 'I . . . I hate to see Iain look like he does.'

Hugh's glance sharpened as he looked at her.

'You like McLaren, don't you, Ailsa?'

She nodded wistfully. 'I can't see that Davina could be other than happy with him. He's a fine man, and he's got the respect of everyone around here.'

He was silent for a while, staring at her thoughtfully

'Well, don't go spending too much of your time over at Cardalloch, will you? You've your own affairs to attend to, your own life to live.'

She laughed. 'You, too?'

'Why, who else said so?'

'Alec McNair. I don't know why you should both grudge me the time I spend keeping Davina's house running for her.'

'Don't you? Maybe we don't grudge it as long as you remember it *is* her house.'

Her eyes sobered. 'What do you mean, Hugh?'

'Nothing . . . I hope. So Alec McNair was advising you as well, was he? Do you like him, too, Ailsa?'

This time she coloured angrily.

'What is this, Hugh, some sort of

third degree? You'll be asking me next when I last saw my father!'

He laughed loudly. 'I'm sorry, Ailsa. Only I've never really agreed with you about marriage between cousins. Lots of couples who are cousins have married, and been happy, and had fine healthy children. Your scruples might do you credit, but I think they're misplaced.'

Ailsa flushed. She had tried to put it out of her mind that ever since she grew up, Hugh had declared himself in love with her, but it kept popping up every now and again. She had always felt, however, that his love did not go very deep.

'Mother would welcome it, too. You know she looks on you as a daughter.'

'It's no good, Hugh. It isn't just that we are cousins, it's the fact that I don't love you enough. If I did, then I would forget that we are cousins. Don't you see that?'

He sighed and nodded.

'You seem very sure now, about not

being in love with me, I mean. You didn't tell me that last time I asked you. Could it now be that you know about falling in love?'

His eyes were searching as he gazed at her, and she turned away.

'Of course not. I don't love anybody. I like being as I am now. The time when women had to be married off quickly, or find a dead-end job, has now gone. A woman can have a rich, full life these days without rushing into marriage.'

Hugh pursed his lips, without comment, though he obviously thought that a pity.

'Leave me telephone numbers where I can reach you quickly, Hugh, in case . . . just in case I want to talk to you.'

He knew what she had in mind, but made no comment as he drew out a notebook and pencil, and wrote them down for her.

'I'm sorry to leave you with all this, Ailsa,' he told her, 'but it is essential that I have to be away from Kilcraig while Father's in America. If you weren't here with Mother, then I suppose I would have to make other arrangements, but I'm very grateful they aren't necessary. I hope you won't be too proud to accept the financial arrangements I've made for you!'

'Oh, Hugh!'

'You must see it from my point of view. I'm depending on you.'

'It's all right, Hugh. Aunt Elizabeth and I understand.'

Gently he drew her into his arms and kissed her. It was not a cousinly kiss.

'Goodbye, my dear. Remember not to do too much, especially for McLaren.

She nodded, but made no comment.

★ ★ ★

Alec McNair rang her up the following day.

'You said you were interested to see how I go about my research?'

'Yes, I did.'

'Well, how are you on climbing?'

She chuckled. 'You, too? Stuart has been coaxing me up to the Falls of Lingarry, and I've promised that we'll trudge up to the Falls of Glomach when his hand is better. It's a better climb for the boy.'

'Well, if you can make that, then you can come with me if you like. John McLean thinks he has seen dotterels nesting at a place he has mapped out for me. I want to take a preliminary look before I set up a hide, and take up all my equipment. We can go quite a way in the Range-Rover, but it might be hard going after that. I would want us to set out early, and I'll pack some food for us both. Good sustaining stuff . . . no fancy sandwiches.'

'I'd like to come, Alec. I'll have to make arrangements at Cardalloch, though.'

She was aware of heavy silence on the other side of the phone.

'Are you sure they can spare you?' he asked dryly.

She bit back a retort, bearing in mind Hugh's advice.

'I'm quite sure they can,' she said equably.

'And you'll be out of bed in time?'

'Now you are being naughty,' she said, though there was a smile in her voice. 'Of course I'll be up and ready.'

He gave her a list of clothing which he advised her to wear, and Ailsa found herself looking forward a great deal to her outing. She liked walking, but when it was a good climb with a purpose at the end of it, then that made it all the more exhilarating.

Next morning her alarm went at five, however, and she rose, bleary-eyed, and put on enough clothes to make her look a stone heavier. She thought, with a small smile, that keeping a date with a man in the country was certainly different from an evening out in town.

Alec greeted her briskly, and ran a bright eye over her approvingly.

'Good girl! You look just fine.'

'All set for the first waltz,' she

grinned, and he looked a trifle uncomprehending, then grinned with her, his eyes crinkling.

'The next time it *will* be the first waltz, Ailsa,' he told her, 'but just now keep hold of this ordnance map, will you? If we can't find the spot John McLean has marked, he'll just have to get time off and give me a bit of guidance. I don't want to bother him just now, though. He's kept busy enough because he doesn't want to bother you or your aunt Elizabeth too much.'

'I didn't know . . . ' she began.

'He can cope,' said Alec briefly. 'John's dependable, so just depend on him. He'd prefer it that way.'

Ailsa nodded silently, accepting that what Alec said was true.

'What kind of bird did you say?' she asked, with interest.

'A dotterel, or at least it will be a pair, because John thinks they are nesting.'

'And they are rare?'

'Yes. Not so very many pairs left in Britain now, and none seen as far west for a while. Usually they breed in the Cairngorms, then they are off south for the winter to North Africa, or around the Red Sea.'

Ailsa sat silent while the car bumped over little more than a track, and listened with interest while Alec told her all he knew about the bird.

'They're a kind of plover,' he continued, 'and of course, like a lot of other birds, they used to get shot to be eaten.'

'Then they are big birds?'

'Not so big. Eight to nine inches. They are interesting in that the female is the brighter bird, while her husband sits on the eggs.' He grinned, glancing at her sideways. 'Maybe you think that is how it should be?'

Her own cheeks dimpled, but she refused to be drawn.

'Anything else?'

'Only that at courting time the female usually takes the initiative.'

116

Again she was aware of laughter in his voice. She was saved from comment as the car stopped, and Alec swung his eyes up over the great hills, with the occasional stretches of marshy ground.

'Sure you can make it, or would you prefer to wait in the car?'

'I'm not sure since I've never tried it, but I'm going to have a jolly good try,' Ailsa informed him, and she was aware of the warmth of his hand on her shoulder, and the flicker of his eyes over her.

'Come on then, Ailsa. Can you carry this haversack while I get on my clobber, binoculars with telescopic lens, camera, notebook and what not.'

'Is that all you need?' she asked. 'I mean does it only take a day to do your research?'

This time he smiled gently.

'Oh, my dear! This is only the preliminary visit. I shall have to make a hide with John McLean's help, and he'll have to leave me at the hide. The birds are wily, and when they see him

117

go, they'll think the coast is clear and I might get some good film.'

'I see,' she said, plunging along by his side. Already the morning air was fresh in her lungs, and she paused to drink in a view of magnificent hills, silvery lochs and clear blue skies. Her body felt strong and young, and she wanted to race ahead buoyantly, but she suspected it might bring unwanted comment from the brisk, purposeful man by her side.

The going became tough, however, and Alec chose a likely spot for a cup of hot coffee and some eggs chopped up in bread rolls which had been thickly buttered, and liberally seasoned. Ailsa did not care for so much pepper, but she was too hungry to criticize and ate with a healthy appetite, finding the strong coffee very good and refreshing.

'Now we take it very easy,' said Alec, studying the map carefully. 'Not far now.'

But it took a great deal of patience and careful searching before Alec finally caught Ailsa's arm and drew her aside as a strange little brown bird with white stripes on its eyes and chestnut breast ran towards them crouching, then flew aggressively, only to flop back on the ground.

Alec had his camera ready and was taking photographs.

'We've disturbed him,' he said quietly.

He quickly photographed the area, deciding where he could make his hide, and Ailsa stood by, silently and respectfully, seeing how thoroughly he undertook his work. There was an air of authority about him which commanded her respect, and she began to see why Davina had also been interested in Alec's work. Fascinated, perhaps? Ailsa found her treacherous thoughts speculating on just what had been between Davina and Alec, then her cheeks coloured, ashamed of those thoughts. She knew that Alec was not the type of man to encourage Davina after her marriage. But what about before she married? Was there anything between them then?

'Ready?' asked Alec, and she started.

'Of course. Any time.'

'I'm sorry.' He grinned at her, his teeth showing white and even. 'Have you been bored, Ailsa?'

'Far from it,' she assured him. 'I was just thinking . . . '

She paused, her cheeks colouring again at the memory of what she had been thinking.

'What?'

'That it was all very interesting,' she ended lamely.

He threw an arm around her shoulder as they started to climb down towards the car and she felt, uncomfortably, the strength of his arm, as well as his personality. He would be a hard man to resist.

She stumbled and his hold tightened. 'Have I tired you, Ailsa?' he asked, his voice suddenly tender, so that her heart jerked.

'Not at all,' she assured him coolly, though keeping a tight hold on herself.

His arm slackened and he swung the haversack off her shoulder.

'I can manage this now.'

'Thank you,' she said formally.

They got back into the car in silence, and he opened the door for her to climb in, after putting his 'clobber' in the boot.

'And now you are back on duty?' he asked heavily.

She flushed. 'Work isn't exactly shameful,' she pointed out.

'Only when it is misplaced.'

'And you think it is?'

'I didn't say so.' His eyes were steely as he turned to look at her before letting in the clutch. 'It's sometimes wise to encourage people to shoulder their own burdens.'

'But surely it's also a kindness to give help where it's needed.'

'So long as you don't allow . . . anyone . . . to depend on you too much. Sometimes stronger feelings can grow out of dependence . . . and . . . out of pity.'

'Did you pity Davina?' she asked sharply.

'I was sorry for her,' he admitted. 'She seemed to lack direction.'

'Which you could have given her?'

'I left that to her husband.'

His voice was dangerously quiet, and when the car finally stopped at Kilcraig, she hardly knew what to say. She knew she had angered him in some way, and felt rather desolate that a beautiful start to the day had somehow been spoiled.

'Thank you for taking me,' she said, with difficulty. 'I . . . I suppose you'll be away now for a while . . . making a hide, as you call it?'

He nodded. 'Yes, I'll be away for a while each day. Cheerio then, Ailsa.'

'Cheerio.'

She had to force back the tears as she walked in the house, but she did not know what was making her heart ache, and decided it was just fatigue. After all, it had been a tough climb for so early in the morning.

5

Lena McLaren began to look a little better as the days passed, and Ailsa saw to it that she had the attention she needed until she was able to sit up, again, on the settee in the drawing room. Ailsa had told her Hugh's ideas about Davina, mainly as a guide in trying to find out if Lena knew why she would just walk out. But although the older woman protested that she knew of no reason, Ailsa could not help feeling that she did have some idea, and was afraid to face up to it.

'And your cousin thinks she will just walk in again one of these days?' she asked Ailsa eagerly.

Ailsa nodded, looking at Lena thoughtfully. There was no doubt in her mind that Mrs McLaren very much wanted to see Davina again, back in her own home.

'He can't believe anything else. She obviously hasn't met with an accident round here, or we would have had word of it by now. Someone was sure to know about it. And there's no girl in any of the hospitals with loss of memory, from what Hugh can find out. Besides, she would have had her identity written down somewhere among her things. Her engagement ring alone is quite distinctive.'

There was more colour in Lena's face, and more life in her as she nodded.

'And she didn't quarrel with you? Or . . . or with Anice?'

This time colour crept into Lena's thin cheeks.

'Not with me. And if Anice and she had quarrelled to that extent, we would all have heard it. Now and again, Anice . . . and Stuart, too, for that matter . . . used to . . . to tease her a little. I stopped them. They were used to the rough and tumble of each other, but Davina's brother is much older than she, and she was brought up almost like an only child, from what I can gather.'

Ailsa nodded. 'Aunt Elizabeth was very protective towards her.'

'Yes. I've tried to explain that to the children, and Anice is . . . well, at a difficult age.'

There was silence between them for a while, neither wishing to discuss Davina's relationship with Iain, which could be most important of all.

'You've made the old house comfortable again, Ailsa,' Lena said at length. 'I'm sure I can take over soon, though we have all been glad of your help meantime.'

'I'm glad to do it,' Ailsa told her.

The door flew open, and Stuart rushed in, his right hand still bandaged, and the bandage looking as black as the boy's knees.

'Ailsa! Ailsa! Can . . . can I take . . . ?'

He paused, his chest heaving, and Ailsa, laughing, made him sit down on a small stool.

'Get your breath back, silly boy,' she chided, 'then tell me what you want. First of all, though, you get a clean bandage. I thought the nurse had dressed your hand.'

'She did,' Lena told her ruefully, 'only Stuart's been out since then.'

'There's no time,' the boy protested. 'Iain can't get home for a bite an' he wants some bread an' a flask.' Stuart got it out almost parrot-fashion. 'He's up in the woods near the old brig with the foresters. I'll take it to him in a basket.'

'You don't go a step till I've cleaned up that bandage,' said Ailsa firmly, 'then I'll pack a basket and we'll both carry it up to Iain. I'm not sure you should be racing around like this.'

Stuart scowled, but he had learned not to argue with Ailsa.

'I'll help him carry the basket.'

Anice sauntered into the room, looking fresh and lovely in the laundered white blouse and the red skirt. She was poor at washing and ironing, except for her own things, and she worked at those carefully till they were perfect. Ailsa glanced at her, and was again struck by the girl's beauty. Yet there was something almost insolent about her at times which jarred.

'You can come, too, if you like,' said Ailsa. 'It's a lovely day, delightful for a walk. I'm sure we'll all enjoy it.'

'But I'm sure you would find lots to do at home,' Anice said sweetly. 'You are always grumbling about having too little time, and this is something I could easily do for you.'

'That's most kind of you, Anice,' said Ailsa, equally sweet, 'but I rather think I would like a walk today. As I say, we can all go.'

Anice's eyes smouldered, but she said nothing more, and Ailsa got Ina Blair to help her pack a basket. She almost expected Anice to back out of going, since she did not get her own way, but the girl was hanging about, along with Stuart who was surveying his new bandage dolefully, obviously in doubt as to how long this one would stay clean.

'We used to come with Davina like this,' said Stuart, as he raced beside Ailsa, while Anice swung along silently. 'We did, didn't we, Anice?'

'Yes,' she said shortly.

'She quite liked doing this, though she hated doing other things.'

'What other things?' asked Ailsa.

'Oh, look, isn't that a squirrel?' cried Anice.

'Where? Where, Anice?' Stuart was a lover of squirrels, and all agog.

'Over there . . . behind that beech tree now.'

'Its tail will be bright orange, won't it, Anice? It gets dark in the autumn.'

Stuart was stalking round towards the tree, but he was disappointed when there was no sign of his favourite wild creature.

'I wish I could make one tame,' he mourned, 'and get it to take nuts out of my hand.'

'It would bite you,' taunted Anice.

'It wouldn't!'

'It would!'

'Wouldn't!'

'Stop quarrelling, both of you,' said Ailsa, and flushed as Anice gave her a sardonic smile. It was difficult not to treat the girl like a child at times, though Anice always succeeded in reminding her that she was a child no longer.

She was about to bring the subject back to Davina, interested to find to just what she hadn't liked to do, when Stuart gave a whoop and ran ahead to where several men were working in among the trees. Iain had already explained how some of the timber had been sold to timber merchants, who were now felling the trees.

Iain was looking better, and Ailsa could not help feeling pleasure and satisfaction as she looked at him. Although he was clad in workmanlike clothes, not so very different from the other men, his shirt was now clean and well pressed, with every button neatly in place, and he wore a fine jersey without holes.

'We've all come,' she announced happily, and saw swift shadow darken his eyes. Too late she remembered that Stuart had told her Davina often used to do this very thing.

Anice was skipping towards him and reaching out to hug him round the waist, as she had no doubt often done as a younger girl.

Almost automatically he put his arm round her and stroked her soft dark hair, while he chatted to Ailsa, and grabbed Stuart, telling him sharply that certain directions were out of bounds.

Ailsa looked on, her eyes drawn to Anice, who was looking at her from under lowered lids. The smile went stiff on Ailsa's face, as she felt a stab of fierce anger, and another emotion which was a little like jealousy, as she looked up at the tall, strong man with the dark, clean-cut face and the lovely clinging girl by his side. Because this was no little sister he was caressing.

This was a young woman, arrestingly beautiful, whose eyes said that she knew exactly what she was doing.

Ailsa caught her own breath, her knees trembling with her own emotions, and her thoughts flew to Davina. Was this, perhaps, the answer to why she had walked out? Had Anice deliberately provoked her jealousy?

But already the scene was changing, and Iain was sitting down and spreading out a napkin while Ailsa automatically began to pour coffee for him, and produced some other light refreshment for the three of them.

'This is good, Ailsa,' Iain told her. 'On a day like this, it saves a great deal of time. Several timber merchants have bought trees, and some supervision is required when felling.'

'I see. Is it all part of your income from the estate, Iain?'

He nodded. 'One has to be skilful in estate management these days, and see that every part of the estate pays for itself, and is used to its best advantage.

You are more fortunate at Kilcraig since your aunt married a wealthy man, with a good business, not dependent on Kilcraig. Don't think I'm just envious of my father-in-law, however. I have great respect for him, and . . . ' Iain paused thoughtfully, 'and, I suppose, sympathy for him, too.'

'Sympathy?'

'It seems sad that he has to go haring off all over the world to earn money to keep it all going, when he could be out here among all this . . . '

He waved his hand at the beautiful scenery around them, and Ailsa nodded, understanding what he meant.

'But if it weren't for him, you might not have married Davina so quickly,' muttered Anice, and Iain's face grew hard and stern as he looked at her.

'You speak in riddles, child.'

'You married her because she was from well-off Kilcraig, and before anyone else could marry . . . '

Furious anger put a mask on Iain's face.

'How dare you, child,' he said icily. 'I have no intention of discussing my wife with you. I married her because I loved her . . . I still love her.'

Ailsa saw the flash of tears in the girl's eyes.

'It was too soon,' she said chokily, and turned to walk away, fumbling for her handkerchief.

Iain's eyes were still flashing for a moment, then he sighed as he turned to Ailsa.

'I think Anice found our short engagement rather bewildering,' he apologised heavily. 'She had a new sister before she had got time to get used to the idea.'

'Didn't Davina object to that, too?' asked Ailsa. 'I mean, isn't it possible that she found Anice's attitude rather . . . hostile?'

'Davina knew she was mistress of her home,' Iain told her coldly. 'If Anice couldn't accept that, then we would have been able to make alternative arrangements. It was Davina's wish, however, that my stepmother and . . . and her family should remain under our roof. I asked her, several times. She was quite vehement that she didn't mind at all.'

'I see,' said Ailsa.

Once again she was feeling bewildered because there was no doubting Iain's sincerity. Almost it seemed, for a moment, that she had an answer to questions which teased her. Almost she believed that it was jealousy of Anice which had driven Davina away.

Yet if she *had* been jealous of Anice, would she not have seized upon Iain's plans to make different arrangements for his stepmother and her family? There was quite a good house near Cardalloch which could have been put into decent repair, and be made into a home for them, but Davina had not accepted this offer.

Iain's black eyes were on her thoughtfully, and she was aware of the power of this man as he sat beside her. Dimly she was also aware of why Hugh, and

Alec McNair, had warned her of the dangers of looking after his household so faithfully. She had to keep a very tight hold on her emotions, and she knew that Anice had guessed this. Perhaps that was why the girl was trying to taunt her a little.

Ailsa pulled herself together with an effort. She would really have to keep a tight hold on herself.

As she repacked the basket, and collected the other two, she smiled calmly at Iain.

'Thank you for coming,' he told her gravely.

'We've all enjoyed it, I'm sure. Come on, Stuart. Oh dear, just *look* at that bandage!'

She ran after Stuart, a laugh sounding behind her, thinking that she had rarely heard Iain laugh since she came. Anice was again swinging along, her red skirt making a splash of colour against the greens and browns of the moorland.

'We'll really have to go out walking again,' she said to the girl, determined to be pleasant. 'I've promised to take Stuart to the Falls of Glomach near Killilan next week. Like to come, Anice?'

'She likes the Falls of Lingarry best,' shouted Stuart. 'Remember, Anice? She wanted Davina to go, but Davina hates going, doesn't she, Anice?'

The girl's face was white and Ailsa thought she was full of temper.

'Shut up, Stuart,' she said furiously. 'I don't want to go climbing anywhere.'

'But you always come. You aren't a fearty. You aren't a fearty-fearty, are you? Neither is Ailsa.'

'Was Davina?' asked Ailsa quietly.

'Sure she was.'

'I'm fed up hearing about Davina,' said Anice, running ahead.

Ailsa grabbed Stuart's good hand.

'Did . . . did anyone look up at the Falls when . . . when Davina went missing?' she asked shakily, fear again taking hold of her, then wished she had not asked the boy such a question. He did not seem at all worried, however.

'Sure they did. The men all looked, though it was a waste of time. She wouldn't have gone, she was so feart.'

Ailsa felt her knees trembling even more with relief. It was exhilarating to climb up and see the huge walls of water thundering over the mountainous rocks, but people had been known to slip and fall . . .

'Race you home,' she said to Stuart, seeing that Anice was now running ahead like a young deer.

'Okay,' he agreed, his brown legs twinkling while she ran lightly, handicapped by the picnic basket.

That night she dreamed she was standing on the edge of the Falls of Lingarry while the water thundered in her ears, and Iain stared across at her from a high boulder. She wanted to jump to him, but Alec grabbed her arm, holding her fast.

Ailsa woke feeling tired and unrefreshed. All of a sudden she wanted to go back to her own quiet, uneventful life in Glasgow where she had enjoyed doing a full-time job in a busy office. Even her small lonely flat seemed attractive.

She came downstairs, wondering if she would find Aunt Elizabeth looking strong enough to be able to leave her, even for just a week. She had given up her job now, but she could still go home to Ayr until she decided whether or not to find another job in Glasgow, or take up Hugh's offer of a post with their firm in Edinburgh. But that, too, might present problems, she thought ruefully.

Aunt Elizabeth was opening the mail, and she turned to Ailsa, tears welling in her eyes.

'Your uncle Robert is on his way home, Ailsa dear. Here, see what he says. It's for you, too.'

Ailsa read the letter a trifle reluctantly, but she saw that her uncle was very relieved to have her beside her aunt at this anxious time, and hoped she would stay till he got home. After which, he thought, stronger measures ought to be taken to find his daughter.

'I'm so glad he's coming home,' said Aunt Elizabeth, and Ailsa had a sudden insight into how hard it had been for her aunt to keep up a brave front. She was glad she had not advocated leaving her just yet.

'So am I,' she said gently.

'You . . . you'll stay till he comes, dear?'

Ailsa sighed a little and nodded. 'Of course.'

'I'm so glad. I . . . I couldn't be by myself. I just couldn't.'

Ailsa let Aunt Elizabeth weep again. It would do her good.

6

Ailsa began to cut down her visits to Cardalloch, feeling that perhaps it was not a good thing for them to become too dependent on her, or for her to go there too often. It seemed, however, that Anice had come to accept her, but was still giving little sign of being overjoyed at having her there.

Time began to hang a trifle heavily on her hands, though, as Aunt Elizabeth was managing to run her own affairs quite well, so that it seemed providential when Alec McNair rang up one evening with a request for her to do a little job for him.

'I thought you were at your hide,' she said, smiling.

She had not seen him since the day he took her out in the Range-Rover.

'I have to come out of it sometimes,' he told her, amused. 'You don't think

I sleep there, do you?'

'No. But . . . '

'I have to go to Inverness for supplies. Would you like to come with me tomorrow? Will Gregg, one of the foresters, is taking over for me for an hour or two, though I think there's a week or so yet before the eggs hatch. I'll want to be on the job constantly then, so I'm stocking up with all I need now.'

'What sort of job would you like me to do for you?' she asked.

'A bit of typing, if you can read my handwriting. I'm afraid my typewriter is a bit ancient, but if I can manage to turn out readable stuff with two fingers, surely a professional like yourself can make some sort of job of it.'

'All right,' she agreed. 'What do I do, where and when?'

'I'll tell you that tomorrow morning about ten, if that's all right.'

'Fine,' she agreed, and put down the receiver, conscious that she was looking forward to this outing to Inverness. She hurried off to find her Aunt Elizabeth.

'Will you be all right if I go with Alec to Inverness?' she asked anxiously.

'Of course I will, dear. As a matter of fact, I'll be glad for you to go, as I have a few things written down on my shopping list for just such an opportunity. Maybe you could get them for me.'

'I'll be delighted,' Ailsa told her happily.

Elizabeth looked at her, and sighed.

'How well you look, Ailsa dear. At least the fresh air round Kilcraig is doing you good.'

Ailsa's cheeks coloured faintly pink. She was feeling very fit, but it made her feel a trifle guilty when she thought of the reason for her visit.

'I've been wondering, Aunt Elizabeth,' she began rather hesitantly, 'when Uncle Robert comes I'd like to go home for a short while, if you don't mind. It seems ages since I saw Mother and Daddy and . . . and the boys.'

Elizabeth's eyes shadowed.

'Of course, my dear. I've no claim on you, you know that, and if you want to go home, do so by all means.'

'Please don't put it like that,' said Ailsa. 'You know I haven't minded staying here with you in the least.'

'I also know that it must be boring here for a young girl like you, and you'll want to get on with your own life.'

'No, it hasn't been boring,' said Ailsa slowly. Her emotions had been too caught up for her to feel bored. There was still the pressing sense of anxiety at the back of her mind, and Cardalloch and its inmates were beginning to make a deep impression on her because she was aware of strange elusive fears, which disappeared as soon as she tried to pinpoint them. She was also deeply aware of McLaren himself, and felt her emotions stirred strongly in ways she was afraid to analyse.

Then there was Alec McNair who also seemed to loom in her life like a large piece of rock which had rolled into her path. Although she had seen little of him, she had been aware of him nearby, and felt that his professional watching eye which could bring the habits of shy wild creatures right into one's own living-room had also been trained on her, and he could see into her very heart.

If she could see into his, she mused, she would no doubt find Davina's interests there. She wanted nothing which belonged to her cousin, but Alec's vigilance was a pinprick to her. She wanted to assure him that her only interest in Cardalloch was a charitable one, but she could see, again, his eyes on her speculatively, eyes which told her they would make up their own mind. Was it really true that he knew nothing of Davina's whereabouts, and why she had just gone away? Could it be that the watchful eye was also protectively on her cousin?

Ailsa rubbed her forehead, feeling her thoughts again churning round and round, so that it was difficult for her to remain clear-headed. There were so very many questions she just could not answer.

★ ★ ★

Ailsa dressed with care next morning, putting on her smartest suit in pale grey, elegantly cut to show her slim figure, her flame-coloured accessories bringing highlights to her russet brown hair and warm apricot skin.

The Range-Rover had been cleaned and polished for its journey to Inverness, and Alec was elegantly dressed in fine Lovat tweeds.

'I hope you're prepared to make a day of it,' he told her, smiling, his blue eyes frankly admiring when she came to meet him. 'I know somewhere where we can have a nice meal and that waltz if we feel so inclined.'

'Won't you have to pick up your assistant at the hide? What was his name?'

'Will Gregg? He's one of the foresters

145

on the Estate, but he's even more knowledgeable about the local wild life than I am. He's got a feeling for birds and animals that's almost . . . well, uncanny, and he knows the whole of this territory so well he could recognise every inch blindfolded. He's got more free time to help me, too, than John McLean.'

'He sounds interesting,' Ailsa remarked, feeling suddenly buoyantly happy as they drove south, past the Five Sisters of Kintail to Invermoriston, where Alec would turn off for Inverness, one of Ailsa's favourite towns.

She wrinkled her brows for a moment.

'Gregg? Will Gregg?'

'His mother was Nanny Gregg in your aunt Elizabeth's household,' Alec enlightened her, and Ailsa laughed with pleasure.

'Of course, Nanny Gregg. I had to ask Bella if she was still alive.'

'She is — very much so. Their cottage used to be a shepherd's cottage, while Will's father was alive, but Will took to forestry instead. He works for Cardalloch, though his mother used to be at Kilcraig.'

'I see,' said Ailsa, then her eyes grew more sober. 'I wonder if old Nanny Gregg heard any rumours about Davina. She might be worrying herself if she has.'

'You can bet that she knows all right,' Alec told her, rather grimly. 'News can travel like wildfire in these parts, and anyway, the foresters will all have heard of it, though Will isn't one to gossip, and keeps his thoughts to himself.'

'So long as Nanny Gregg doesn't get upset,' murmured Ailsa. 'She's a dear old soul.'

'She sends you her love, anyway.' Alec told her, smiling, 'and a warm invitation to tak' a wee walk her way as soon as you're able. Will is going to bring you the message.'

'I'll do that,' Ailsa nodded, 'only I'm going home for a week or so when Uncle Robert comes back. I want to see

Mum and Dad again, and the boys.'

'I'm glad to hear it,' Alec told her simply. 'It's good to know Cardalloch can get on without you for a wee while.'

The tone had been light, but Ailsa flushed, sensing more purpose behind the words.

'What I do for Cardalloch is my own affair,' she said coldly, her chin lifting. 'I think I'm the best judge of how much to do, or . . . or how little.'

'Don't start getting on your high horse again,' Alec told her, with a hint of exasperation. 'I only . . .'

'Wanted to give me good advice,' finished Ailsa. 'Why does everyone try to advise me? Am I not capable of looking after my own affairs?'

'I see that you *think* you are,' Alec told her quietly. 'We'll say no more about it, though the way you fly to McLaren's defence would arouse anybody's suspicions.'

'Of what?'

'Of . . . your regard for him, perhaps?'

Hot colour was tingling her cheeks. 'That's a horrible thing to say! You forget he's married to my cousin.'

'I hadn't forgotten.'

'I might have known not to come with you, even for the day. You're so . . . so irritating!'

'And you've dark red hair, and that should be a warning to anybody not to say a word out of turn,' he said ruefully. 'Suppose we call a truce for the rest of the day. See, there's Loch Ness now. It's too far to drive you all the way back to Kilcraig.'

'All right,' she conceded, rather grudgingly, wondering why this man could rouse her so quickly to anger. She hated to see the amused laughter in his blue eyes, as though he could see so much more than she could, and was watching her live her life like a game of chess where a single move on his part could have her in check.

'I hope you'll be able to do that typing before you go,' he told her mildly. 'It's an article, and I like to have my final copy neatly typed.'

'Who usually does it?' she asked curiously.

'I send it away.'

'And you can't this time?'

'My typist has a three-week delay. I don't want to wait that long. Will usual rates do?'

'No,' she said, offended. 'Of course I'll do it for you for . . . for . . .'

'Love?'

The gleam was back in his eyes and she felt her heart leap, then begin to pound madly to her considerable annoyance. Alec McNair had a very odd effect on her, she thought, her cheeks again warm with colour.

'I should be happy to do it for you out of friendship,' she said primly, and he gave a hoot of laughter.

'Nevertheless, my dear Ailsa, I asked you to do this work for me, and I intend to pay you standard rates. Is it agreed?'

They were coming to the outskirts

of Inverness, and she nodded.

'It's agreed, though by that measure I ought to be paying half the petrol money for our shopping expedition.'

The car had stopped, and steely fingers gripped her arm.

'Now you've said enough, my dear,' he told her quietly. 'I asked you to accompany me because I wanted you with me. Do you understand that?'

Again her heart leapt, and she nodded.

'We'll have a quick lunch, then do our respective shopping, then we're free to enjoy ourselves. O.K?'

Her eyes were suddenly shy as she nodded again.

'Okay, Alec,' she said softly.

* * *

It seemed hours later when Ailsa and Alec were once again in the car, speeding smoothly into the quiet of a summer evening. It had been a wonderful day, thought Ailsa rather tiredly, though her fatigue was pleasant and relaxing.

She had spent an hour or two shopping and had met Alec again at a prearranged time, when he drove out to a charming hotel where a table had been booked for them both.

'I should have dressed up,' she said, looking round.

'Nonsense,' Alec told her, 'and I'm not going to pay you compliments in case all those prickles come out again. But we can dance without being in evening dress, can't we?'

Apparently they could, and Ailsa relaxed and began to enjoy herself thoroughly, acutely conscious of Alec as he danced lightly and gracefully for such a big man.

'You're like a piece of thistledown,' he told her.

'It's easy to dance with you,' she said frankly.

'My mother saw to it that I was taught the social graces,' Alec told her, grinning.

'Your . . . mother?'

'I've lost both parents,' he told her flatly.

'Of course. I . . . I'm sorry.'

'It was a long time ago,' he explained quietly. 'Nevertheless, I envy you your happy family.'

'Yes, I am lucky,' she said seriously. 'Perhaps . . .'

'Yes?'

'Nothing really.'

'No, finish what you were going to say.'

She was a trifle embarrassed. 'I was just wondering if you would care to come and meet my family in Ayr some time.'

'That would be delightful,' Alec told her, and there was no doubt that he meant it. 'I think I remember your mother, as a matter of fact, though I was a very young boy when she married.'

'It is a happy marriage,' Ailsa told him, rather stiffly.

'I'm sure of it. They have produced

you, haven't they?'

Once again the blue eyes were gleaming, and she felt the prickles coming out, but he must have seen the danger signals because he swung her into the dance, then led her back to their table, flushed and breathless.

Now they sat side by side in the Range-Rover while Alec guided it gently along the road skirting the most famous loch in the country, which now looked beautifully peaceful in the quiet of evening.

'Isn't it all beautiful?' asked Ailsa. 'I can feel the beauty so much that it tingles the palms of my hands.'

'You're a strange girl, Ailsa,' Alec told her, in an odd voice. 'Strange, but different.'

'I'm very ordinary,' she told him, smiling. 'I was never allowed to get uppity, or my brothers cut me down to size.'

'Then you're even more fortunate than you know. It would be valuable training for many of us.'

The moonlight was bathing the countryside in its queer ghostly light as Alec drove the car north towards Dornie, and took a high road so that they could look down on Eilean Donan Casle, the loch shimmering around it, and the dark mountains behind, with the sky still glowing richly red and orange.

'Sometimes it doesn't seem real,' said Ailsa, in an awed voice.

'But it is. It's like some moments in our lives, which don't seem real either.'

He turned her to him and kissed her gently, then pulled her into the full strength of his arms, and for her the moment seemed to be carved out of time.

Then he released her, and she sat stiffly beside him, hardly able to think.

'Don't I even get my face slapped?' he asked, and she knew the laughter would be back in his eyes, so that slow anger began to burn. She fought to keep cool, however.

'You said it was a moment in our lives which wasn't real,' she reminded him, and heard him catch his breath, then sigh deeply.

'Yes, I did say that, didn't I? Come on, then, Ailsa. I'd better get you home. That, at least, is very real.'

She nodded dumbly, ashamed to realise that tears were pricking her eyelids. Luckily, when they eventually reached Kilcraig, Alec was too busy helping to sort out her items of shopping to notice.

But that night Ailsa's normally healthy sleep was very disturbed, and her bed grew lumps as hard as bricks. She knew that Alec McNair's kiss had stirred her as no kiss had ever stirred her before, but beyond that she did not wish to investigate.

As he had explained to her, all work and no play was a very true saying, and especially so when he was engaged in such absorbing work as he was doing at the moment.

And tonight she had been part of

the 'play', to be laid aside like a fluffy rabbit or a coloured ball, in the hands of a small boy. Next time Alec McNair would have to find someone else to have fun with, she thought, a sob suddenly catching her throat. For her the 'unreal' moment had been very real indeed.

7

Uncle Robert came home a few days later looking tired and drawn, even if he declared his business trip to be highly successful. It would have been more enjoyable, however, if Aunt Elizabeth had been with him.

'And you haven't heard from the child?' he asked heavily. 'What is McLaren thinking about to let her stay away without finding out her whereabouts? And what about Hugh? Why hasn't he done something about it?'

'They've both done their best, Uncle Robert,' defended Ailsa.

She had talked it all over again with Iain the previous day, when she told him she hoped to go home for a week or two.

'Surely Davina will have become homesick by then,' she told him, 'and

I can start looking for another job. Hugh wants me to go to Edinburgh, but I don't know . . . '

Her words had been a trifle heedless as she saw by the bleak expression on his face when she had referred to Davina's being homesick, and again she felt angry with her cousin for causing so much heartache. She would have supposed Davina to be heartsick, as well as homesick, with someone like Iain McLaren to care for her.

'Is there still no word?' she asked softly, and he shook his head.

'I've been to the police,' he said flatly, 'but apparently young women leave home every day for reasons best known to themselves. It would be different in the case of . . . ' he hesitated, 'foul play, as they put it. However, so far they don't suspect me of doing away with my wife.'

Ailsa was silenced by the harsh tone in his voice, and by the horror conjured up by his words. She shivered even though she knew there was no reason to suspect foul play.

'You'll be all right for a week or two?' she asked, briskly matter-of-fact. 'Lena seems much better now.'

Ailsa hoped Mrs McLaren was better, though once or twice she had thought the older woman's newfound energy seemed a trifle feverish.

Iain nodded, his eyes gentler as they rested on her.

'I can't thank you enough, Ailsa. I've . . . I've rather selfishly taken up your time. I believe you're also working for McNair?'

She coloured under his gaze.

'Only to type out an article for him.'

'I see. He's an interesting man. Davina found him . . . er . . . interesting to talk to.'

'Yes.' She hesitated for a moment. 'I'm sure he has nothing to do with her going away.'

He turned quickly, a flash of something in his eyes, though she found it hard to tell what he was thinking.

'Of course,' he told her politely.

'I'll call and see you again, when I come back,' she assured him. 'I'll just say goodbye to Stuart, and Anice.'

Stuart looked rather huffed when he knew she would not be back for a week or two, though Anice did not even try to conceal her delight.

'My hand will soon be better, well enough for climbing, and you promised to take me up to the Falls of Lingarry. I want Anice to go, but she won't.'

'I'm fed up squelching up there,' said Anice, sharply, 'and anyway, you were going to Glomach, not Lingarry.'

'Lingarry makes a tougher climb,' insisted Stuart.

'Well, I've written home now,' apologised Ailsa, 'and my parents are expecting me.'

'You need a break,' Anice told her, her voice becoming friendly with the relief she so obviously felt. Ailsa looked at her curiously.

'You haven't really liked me coming over here, have you, Anice?' she asked deliberately.

The girl flushed and looked away.

'Why should Iain get you to boss us all about?' she asked sulkily. 'I'm old enough to take Dav . . . Mother's place now.'

'You should have made a better job of it,' said Ailsa mildly.

'I did. I was. Only Iain wouldn't give me time. And he knows I'm not a little girl any longer.'

Again there was the sunny look on her face, and a sideways glance for the older girl. But Ailsa had grown rather tired of Anice's moods.

'I'll just go and find your mother,' she said briskly. ' 'Bye for now. I'll probably see you both shortly after I get back.'

'And go that climb? To Glomach?'

'To Glomach,' she assured Stuart, and turned to Anice who was smiling happily.

'Goodbye, Ailsa,' she said sweetly. 'Don't hurry back.'

* * *

But now Uncle Robert was pacing up and down, asking questions, and weighing up the answers.

'If she hadn't married McLaren, I'd have been away thumping on McNair's door. He would soon take her in if he thought she was unhappy, but he is as old-fashioned as they come, and there would have been his wedding ring on her finger, not McLaren's.'

Ailsa felt her mouth go dry, and felt bound to agree with Uncle Robert's assessment.

'They were all an honourable lot, the McNairs. Maybe that's why Alec's home is now a cottage.'

'It's all he needs,' flashed Ailsa. 'It's a lovely cottage.'

'But hardly like his old home,' Uncle Robert told her dryly.

'Well, it's no use speculating and wrangling,' put in Aunt Elizabeth. 'She must have gone to a girl friend when she hasn't asked for more clothes to be sent on. And if she had been cashing cheques for new things, no doubt Iain would have heard about it. No, she must be living in with somebody.'

Ailsa merely nodded. They kept going over the same old ground, she thought, rather tiredly. It was one reason why she wanted so much to get away.

'Well, I hope Cardalloch keeps her in better order when she does come back,' Uncle Robert said, rather grimly. 'And you're going to leave us, too, Ailsa?'

'Only for a week or two,' she assured him. 'You know where to find me, if you need me at all.'

'Ailsa could do with getting away from us all,' Aunt Elizabeth said kindly.

'Of course. Of course.'

Ailsa escaped and made her way up to bed. She felt tired and confused, feeling that there was a possibility she had not yet explored, but was unable to pinpoint what it was. Somewhere someone knew more about Davina than they cared to say, but she could not think clearly who it could be. Perhaps it would all fall into place when she took a fresh look at it from her home in Ayr.

* * *

Ailsa did not see Alec again before she left Kilcraig to drive south to Ayr, and she was rather disappointed that he had not got in touch with her.

Hector Donaldson, who knew quite a lot about cars, had checked over her small Mini and pronounced it fit for the journey.

'Mind how you go, though, Miss Ailsa,' he warned. 'I've seen some young lassies like yourself driving these wee cars wi' madness in their hearts.'

Ailsa grinned. 'I'm no speed merchant, Hector. Don't worry.'

'And you'll be back again soon, miss?' he asked, his bright black eyes suddenly anxious.

'Of course, Hector,' she smiled. 'I'll just say goodbye to my aunt and uncle.'

'Give Janet my . . . my love,' said Aunt Elizabeth when she went to find her in the drawing room. 'And James.'

'All right, Aunt Elizabeth. I . . . I'll probably see you soon again.'

'If Davina decides to walk in again, you may want to see her anyway, to find out all about it,' Aunt Elizabeth said, briskly matter-of-fact.

'Yes,' said Ailsa, rather lamely.

Nevertheless she enjoyed the journey south, along good roads with wonderful views of loch and mountain, deciding to pull in at a delightful lay-by by the side of Loch Lomond, and eat the delicious chicken sandwiches which Bella had prepared for her.

It was late afternoon by the time she drove in the narrow drive of her own home, a small villa on the southern outskirts of Ayr, and sudden fatigue brought tears to her eyes as her mother ran out to welcome her.

Janet Kennedy was not at all like her older sister Elizabeth, being small and plump, with pretty soft brown hair.

She was a gentle woman, full of good, sound common sense, and Ailsa was thankful to have her mother's placid ways and her father's quiet reasoning with her again. It was even a delight to hear her small brothers squabbling, and she spared a thought for young Stuart who had few boys to wrangle with while he was off school.

'I should have brought young Stuart home with me,' she told her mother regretfully.

'No, you need a rest, my dear. I can see signs of strain in your face, even if your normal health is obviously very good, and I've no doubt Elizabeth is every bit as bad. She's the one who needs a break, but I don't suppose wild horses would drag her from Kilcraig at this time.'

Ailsa shook her head slowly.

'And poor Iain McLaren, too. He's a fine man, but he does far more thinking than speaking.'

Ailsa smiled a little, agreeing with her mother. Iain was inclined to go off into a world of his own.

'I bet he didn't tell Davina he loved her half often enough,' went on Janet. 'He would expect her to know that, and she's the sort who has to keep being told.'

Ailsa felt taken aback, wondering if her mother's guess was right. Had Davina, somehow, got the idea that Iain did not really love her enough?

'She'd run to her mother,' she said, and Janet shook her head.

'She might not. There was a queer sort of pride in her, and Elizabeth would be all set to do battle. I bet she only intended to go for a weekend, then time would go on and she is now ashamed to come home. Sometimes people put off doing things for a wee while, then they never get them done, because they're ashamed of the delay.'

'I expect you're right, Mother,' Ailsa told her, 'but I think that's too simple. I can't see Davina doing such a thing.'

'Maybe it's your turn to be right,

168

dear,' Janet conceded, 'though I don't blame Elizabeth for being so worried. If it were you, I'd be out of my mind, too. Only . . .'

Janet broke off, casting a look at her daughter. If it were Ailsa, she would have had more sense!

'Tell me about Alec McNair,' she commanded, and her eyebrows lifted a little when she saw the warm colour creep into Ailsa's cheeks.

'He's filming a dotterel which is nesting near Cardalloch, or rather, a pair of dotterels. I believe it isn't usual to find them there. I . . . er . . . I've typed some notes for him.'

'And you found that interesting?'

'Very. He's . . . a very interesting person,' said Ailsa, rather slowly.

'And you've become friends with him?'

Ailsa was direct in giving her answer.

'Friends. Nothing more.'

Janet was just as direct.

'Would you like it to be anything more, Ailsa?'

The girl was silent, then she shook her head.

'I don't know. I . . . I think he was in love with Davina, only she married Iain McLaren. And one can't fall out of love so easily, can one?'

'No,' Janet agreed, her eyes rather troubled. She loved her daughter and wanted to see her happy. There would be no great happiness in falling in love with someone who had given his heart elsewhere.

Ailsa spent a few days trying to relax, going for solitary walks over the Low Green or sitting watching the crowds of early summer visitors on the sands. Sometimes she took the boys, Pat and Tommy, along with her and sometimes it was her father, quietly smoking his pipe, who was happy to be her companion.

Yet the days did not bring order to her confused mind. She found herself worrying about Kilcraig and Cardalloch, seeing Iain's brooding eyes resting on her appealingly, and the defiant Anice, trying to keep her away, while Stuart wanted her to accompany him on all his manly pursuits, no doubt feeling the strong need for companionship.

Had Iain taken him out, wondered Ailsa, before he married Davina? Had the small boy been jealous of his young sister-in-law, and was that why he seemed scornful of her soft gentleness? Perhaps Iain no longer went climbing or fishing without Davina, and Stuart had tried to taunt her into doing everything so that he could still have Iain by his side. It was a theory, thought Ailsa, even if a bit far-fetched.

Then there was Anice, who could climb and run over the hills like a young deer. Yet Anice was so busy showing everyone that she was now grown up that she refused to behave like a young girl.

And Alec McNair? Ailsa's heart beat more strongly when she thought of the enchantment which his companionship had brought as they sat looking down

171

on Eilean Donan in the moonlight. Their moment stolen from time had been like a precious jewel, a moment which she could share with no one, not even her mother.

'Is it a problem, Ailsa?' James Kennedy asked gently, hearing her small sigh.

'It is, rather,' she confessed with a wry smile.

'Problems do sort themselves out, darling,' he told her gently.

She nodded. Only people sometimes got hurt, she thought wistfully, and this time it looked like a few people would be hurt unless Davina decided to come home soon.

* * *

The following day was Sunday, and Ailsa was astonished when a car drove up to the door just shortly before lunch.

'You've got visitors, Mum,' she said, glancing out of the window.

'*We've* got visitors,' her mother corrected, rather dryly. 'It's your cousin Hugh.'

She had never got on very well with her sister's only son. As a small boy he had amused, rather than annoyed her with his bossy attitude, and it had tended to grow with the years.

'Ah, Ailsa, my dear,' he greeted his cousin, after kissing his aunt's cheek. 'Mother said you were here, so I thought I'd drive down and see you. There's much we have to discuss.'

'Then . . . there's no word?' For a moment Ailsa's heart had leapt with hope at the sight of him.

'No. She's being very thoughtless indeed. But I'm going to persuade Mother to come to Edinburgh for a few days, when Father returns to the office. I'm sure the Donaldsons can be trusted to look after things in her absence, and John McLean can manage the estate.'

'It would be a good break for Aunt Elizabeth,' Ailsa agreed.

'Only if you came, too,' Hugh told her eagerly. 'You can be of great help in the office, Ailsa, and . . . well . . . '

He glanced round. There was no good discussing his own future, and Ailsa's, with Aunt Janet showing so much interest. Yet Ailsa was looking specially lovely with the soft colour of summer in her face, and her russet brown hair falling to her shoulders in a soft cloud. She had the sort of warmth and beauty which Hugh had failed to find in any other girl.

'I've been . . . well, planning to go up to Glasgow to see my old firm,' she said hesitantly, 'and the lease of my flat is still paid for a week or two yet.'

'Yes, I was meaning to ask about that,' Janet put in. 'I don't suppose Davina is borrowing the flat, until you return, I mean. She could have been somewhere else in Glasgow, then she could have gone to the flat after you left for Kilcraig.'

Ailsa's eyes were wide, and she looked at Hugh.

'I never thought of that,' she said, sudden excitement in her eyes. 'Oh, Hugh, couldn't we go in your car? I won't rest now till we find out. Oh, Mother, what a brilliant idea!'

'Well, don't build on it,' said Janet flatly, 'and you don't go a step, either of you, till you have had some lunch.'

It was one of their usual delightful Sunday lunches, but Ailsa found difficulty in eating it. New hope was gripping her, and her cheeks were flushed with excitement.

As Hugh installed her comfortably in his big car, however, she could not help remembering how she had gone on another hopeful journey, with Alec over to Kyleakin on Skye, where she had been almost afraid to check up on the hotel which Alec knew had been a favourite with Davina.

In spite of her disappointment, Alec had been there, like a rock. But now it was Hugh, so sure of himself, and so sure that he knew best what she needed in life.

Yet he must be just as anxious as she, Ailsa thought, glancing at his profile. Davina was his sister, and in his own way he loved her very much.

Ailsa could scarcely run up the stairs when they eventually reached her Glasgow address, fumbling in her handbag for her keys. She could not even remember giving one to Davina, but it was quite possible that she had.

A rush of cold air came to meet her, however, and she stood looking round, feeling sick with disappointment. The flat was still neat, and rather sterile in its orderliness. There was no evidence of Davina's presence at all, and Ailsa shivered, so that she felt Hugh's arm on her shoulders, holding her close.

'It was a good try,' he told her, his voice unusually gentle. 'I'm disappointed too, Ailsa.'

She nodded, not trusting herself to speak, then began to walk round the flat, lifting cushions and throwing them down. How small and poky it seemed after the weeks she had spent at

Kilcraig among the freedom of wild mountainous country.

'Would it hurt you to give it up, Ailsa?' Hugh asked her. 'You said you were proud of it.'

'I was,' she admitted. 'No, I . . . I can give it up.'

'Then come to Edinburgh instead.'

She looked round again, hesitating. The flat had one thing Edinburgh might lack. It had independence, *her* independence.

As though reading her thoughts, Hugh hastened to reassure her.

'It will be a job,' he said briskly. 'Well enough paid, but you'll be expected to earn your money. We have a flat there, as you know, but you could always find your own accommodation, and call in to see Mother as you wish. She won't be lonely either. She has plenty of friends in Edinburgh.'

Ailsa nodded, thinking that what Hugh said was sensible.

'I can arrange it for you, then you needn't go back to Kilcraig. You can come straight to Edinburgh, in say, another week? Would that suit you, Ailsa?'

She nodded again, rather tiredly.

'I suppose so, Hugh. Maybe that would be best.'

Yet as they drove back to Ayr, where Janet was insisting that Hugh stay the night, Ailsa felt more than usually depressed. It was not only worry about Davina, and heartfelt sympathy for Iain McLaren, it was the knowledge that if she went to Edinburgh, she might not see Alec McNair again for a long time.

And even if Alec was never likely to fall in love with her, the thought of not seeing him gave her a cold hard pain in her heart. She knew, now, that it was Alec McNair she had fallen in love with, and that this surging emotion was something much stronger than she had ever felt for anyone else, ever before.

8

Ailsa spent a few days going up to Glasgow and removing her personal belongings from the flat. She looked round with regret, feeling that part of her life had closed behind her, yet the future was hardly bright and promising. It was as though she stood at a crossroads where the way which beckoned to her was forbidden, the other uncertain.

'I'll travel up to Edinburgh on Friday,' she told her mother, 'then I'll have the weekend for settling in.'

Hugh had already found accommodation for her within easy reach of their flat and office, and she brightened a little. She loved Edinburgh, too, and in many ways it would be attractive to her to work there.

On Thursday morning, however,

Janet came to tell her that Iain McLaren was on the telephone.

'Iain?' asked Ailsa, with surprise and a quick flash of hope in her eyes. 'Perhaps he's had news of Davina.'

She hurried to lift the receiver, hearing Iain's deep voice on a line which was not too clear.

'Hello, Ailsa?'

'Yes?'

'I got your number from my mother-in-law. Look, my dear, I've no right to ask it of you, but I wondered if . . . if you could come to Cardalloch for a few days again?'

'Come? To Cardalloch?'

'Yes.'

There was silence for a moment.

'Lena's taken ill again. She's collapsed and has had to be put to bed. I . . . I'm trying to find someone I can rely on, but it's taking time and Nurse McCall can only come in daily. I'm . . . concerned for my stepmother and the children.'

Ailsa did not hesitate.

'Of course I'll come, Iain,' she told him quickly. 'Will tomorrow do, if I leave early? I'd better have a word with my uncle and aunt, too . . . and my cousin Hugh.'

'Tomorrow will do fine.'

She could hear the relief in his voice as he thanked her, and she turned to her mother as she put up the receiver.

'There's trouble at Cardalloch, Mummy. Lena McLaren has been taken ill again. I'm not surprised. There was something sort of . . . brittle . . . about her. I think I'd better go and see how things are.'

Janet looked at her speculatively, but said little. It was Hugh who said it all, when Ailsa rang up later.

'But you *can't* go there, Ailsa! You're coming here to me, in Edinburgh. McLaren can get somebody else.'

'That's not so easy at short notice,' defended Ailsa. 'I might not be there long, Hugh. It depends on how bad Mrs McLaren is.'

181

'What about her daughter?'

'Anice is far too young to cope. You know that, Hugh.'

She could hear his deep breathing and sensed anger in him.

'This is just another instance of Davina's selfishness,' he said, after a while. 'If she hadn't walked out on her responsibilities, she would have been there to organise proper nursing for her mother-in-law.'

'And I would still have been working in Glasgow, at my old job,' Ailsa pointed out. 'And don't go blaming Davina till we hear from her again.'

'I suppose you're right,' conceded Hugh, 'but I never understood why you kept passing up a fine chance like the one I'm offering you.'

'Didn't you?'

'Well, you're very stubborn, Ailsa. I've told you that before. Don't let McLaren start claiming your time. You've got your own life to live.'

'Sometimes we've got to give our

time to helping others,' Ailsa said slowly.

'I expect Mother will stay at Kilcraig now,' Hugh told her moodily. 'If you're too long at Cardalloch, I'll come up and have a word with you.'

'I shall plan out my own time,' Ailsa said quietly. 'I'm sorry to have upset your arrangements, Hugh.'

'So am I,' he told her, and hung up.

Ailsa made good time on her journey north again, but when she arrived at Cardalloch, she found the old house back to its neglected-looking and cheerless state again.

Lena McLaren was in bed, looking very pale and ill, while Anice was far from being the flamboyant young woman Ailsa had seen when she was last here. She looked very young again, her face pale and frightened, and she wore her old skirt and blouse instead of her usual colourful clothes.

Stuart looked neglected and dirty, with an unmended tear in his jersey, and his toe peeping through a pair of old plimsolls. McLaren himself was due home at any time, according to Ina Blair.

'I do my best, Miss Ailsa,' Ina complained, 'but you never know where you are among all of them.'

Ailsa felt anger stirring. Ina was a poor worker unless under direction. She had been disappointed, too, to find that Ina had no hidden secrets about Davina, a conclusion she had reached after the most careful questions.

Now she drew a deep breath and began to tell the other woman what to do.

'We'll need two extra women from the village this time,' she decided, 'and I'll see what has to be done about nursing Mrs McLaren.'

In this she had the help of Anice who, for the first time, genuinely welcomed having Ailsa in the house, giving her directions.

'You can work with Nurse McCall,' decided Ailsa. 'She'll tell you what to do.'

The young girl's eyes were red-rimmed, as though she had been crying, and Ailsa impulsively put a hand on her arm.

'Don't worry. She'll be all right,' she said sympathetically. 'Dr Baird seems to think it's mainly nervous exhaustion.'

Anice nodded, her eyes brooding.

'Could it be with . . . with worrying?' she asked, half hesitantly.

'Was she worrying that much?' asked Ailsa. 'Was it about anything special? Davina's absence?'

The dark eyes were frightened as they looked into hers.

'I think she was worrying.'

'Then we'll have to keep trying to locate Davina,' Ailsa comforted. 'Try to keep her cheered up, Anice.'

Next day Ailsa went over to Kilcraig for a quick word with her Aunt Elizabeth.

'I hope you had a nice break, dear,' her aunt said, looking at her solicitously. 'It seems rather much, though, that you've been called back to Cardalloch.'

Ailsa shrugged.

'Iain needs help,' she said simply, and Elizabeth frowned again.

'Alec McNair wanted your address in Ayr, or your telephone number, but I preferred not to give it. I explained that you were getting away from everything for a little while.'

Ailsa's eyes were wide, then she flushed.

'You could at least have asked me, Aunt Elizabeth,' she said, with annoyance. 'I wouldn't have minded hearing from Alec.'

'I don't trust that young man,' her aunt said, rather sullenly. 'Robert thinks he's all right, but he's the only one Davina used to see, apart from Iain, in this district. I don't suspect him of taking her anywhere, but I think he has an idea where she might be. He was very ill at ease with me.'

'Nonsense,' said Ailsa sharply. 'Of course Alec won't be keeping such a thing from you. He knows too well how worried you are.'

'Then why was he so guarded when he talked to me?'

Ailsa wanted to say that it was all Aunt Elizabeth's imagination, but decided that such a comment would hardly be welcome. Yet it wasn't like her aunt to be so imaginative. Perhaps Alec really had been ill at ease with her, though why she had no idea.

Nevertheless it was annoying to know that Alec had wanted to get in touch with her, and had been unable to do so. If it had not been for Iain asking her back, she might have gone to Edinburgh, and become completely out of touch with him.

And now her heart was beating quickly at the thought of seeing him again, soon. Yet it was only her own feelings which had suddenly become clear to her. There was no reason why Alec should have changed.

That evening she decided to walk over to the cottage, after the high tea which Iain preferred to dinner, unless guests were expected. The nights were longer now, and she knew he would still be busy at the hide, until his young birds were ready to leave their home.

'I'll have to spend about four weeks filming from the time they hatch,' he had explained earlier. 'Watching their development is one of the most fascinating aspects of the job.'

'Shall I be able to see the film later?' she had asked, and he grinned.

'Why not? Though, of course, a lot of work will require to be done on it.'

Now she allowed the warm summer air of early evening to fan her cheeks, and lift her long chestnut hair from the back of her neck, as she walked along, clad in a stylish trouser suit which had brought a spark of interest into Anice's eyes.

Smoke was curling from the cottage chimney, and Ailsa went to knock on the door, then tapped at the kitchen window. She saw Alec glance out, then he came to the door, having changed his boots for old carpet slippers, and his jacket for a thick brown sweater. His blue eyes surveyed her solemnly.

'So you've decided to come back?'

'May I come in, Alec?' she asked, and he nodded and invited her into the warmth of his living-room.

'I . . . er . . . I'm sorry Aunt Elizabeth didn't give you my telephone number,' she said hesitantly.

'It's all right, I understood. Mind if I go on cooking my supper? I've only just got home.'

'Here, let me!'

'No, you sit still. You can have a cup of tea,' he told her, pouring thick black tea into a large mug, and spooning in sugar and milk.

Ailsa took it with a word of thanks, looking up at him nervously. If only he would smile at her with the old cheerful grin, or look at her with a softening in his eyes. But she could sense the barrier which had seemed to spring up between them, and her heart sank. Perhaps he had guessed at her feelings for him, and was doing his best to keep her at arm's length. Perhaps that was the reason for his awkward approach to Aunt Elizabeth. Yet if that was so, why had he bothered to try to ring her at all? And it was only since she left Kilcraig that she realised her own feelings for him.

'Why did you want me, Alec?' she asked, after a while.

'No reason. Just to find out why you didn't bother to see me before you left . . . why you ignored my message.'

'What message?'

He looked at her searchingly.

'Oh well, maybe it doesn't matter now. I believe you're going to work in Edinburgh.'

'I was. But I'm at Cardalloch at the moment.'

'Cardalloch?' His eyebrows shot up.

'Yes. Iain rang me at home to tell me his step-mother was ill, so I've come up to see to things until . . . well, until she's better.'

'I see. Davina won't need to hurry back, then.'

Ailsa flushed, then went white.

'That's a rotten thing to say!'

'Well, it strikes me that there's something funny going on,' Alec said, his eyes sparkling blue lights. 'You're very ready to run as soon as McLaren beckons. I notice your telephone number was available to him even if you were supposed to be getting away from it all.'

Ailsa's cheeks were now scarlet with anger.

'What's got into you, Alec McNair?' she asked furiously. 'If you must know, Aunt Elizabeth thinks *you* might know where Davina is.'

'I wish I did,' he told her fervently. 'I think if she's been unhappy with McLaren, she should be given a chance to get out of it. What are his ideas on divorce, Ailsa? Come to that, what are yours?'

She felt as though her heart was tearing as she stood up. So Alec now wanted Davina to get a divorce! Now she really did know why he was so uncomfortable when facing Aunt Elizabeth. It was also one point where she and Alec were going to differ greatly.

'You run your life, Alec. I'll run mine,' she said, roughly, feeling that the tears were not far away. 'I'm sorry I . . . I interrupted your supper.'

'So am I, if it means depriving McLaren of your attention,' he told her, and she could see the anger in him, almost as though he wanted to shake her.

Ailsa left then, walking back quickly through the still-warm evening, the trees swaying gently, and alive with night sounds. The midge repellant she always used was beginning to wear off, and she had not brought her spray, so she slapped at the midges as she walked, making her feel even more cross and miserable.

She could feel the resentment which Alec McNair seemed to be building up against Iain McLaren, and which seemed to have multiplied since she last saw him.

Ailsa swallowed. She had wanted Davina to come home so much, but what would happen when she did? Would Iain McLaren lose her to Alec McNair? Ailsa's mind shied away from divorce as she thought about Iain, and her aunt and uncle. Such a thing would be a bitter blow to all of them, yet it might have to be faced when Davina came home.

* * *

On Friday Ailsa took some time off to keep her promise to Stuart, and take him up to the Falls of Glomach. The school was now on holiday, and the small boy was inclined to be restless, especially when he found the fishing poor.

'Anice can come, too,' he decided,

193

pulling on a strong pair of boots.

'No,' said Anice sharply. 'I don't want to come.'

'But you always come!' he protested.

'Mother needs me.'

'It won't take such a long time,' said Ailsa, 'and your mother sleeps most of the afternoon. I'm sure Ina can keep an eye on her, if you would like a break.'

But the girl shook her head quickly. 'No, thanks.'

'Och, she's no fun any more,' said Stuart disgustedly. 'Shall I get in the car, Ailsa?'

'Yes. I'll just get some sandwiches and hot coffee in a haversack.'

Ailsa drove carefully up the narrow road which skirted Loch Long, and on to the Killilan Estate, where they were given the courtesy of using a private road, which was rather rough going in parts.

'We've got to sign the visitors' book,' cried Stuart. 'Haven't we, Ailsa?'

'All right,' she laughed, and followed

him out of the car to sign the book, which was kept on a table outside the gates of the house.

It was now a busy season for visitors and Stuart was eager to look at all the names of people who had come from all over the world.

'Come on,' said Ailsa. 'We'd better go now, Stuart.'

In a flash he was back in the car, chattering like a small monkey, while Ailsa negotiated the bumpy road for a few more miles, till they came to the parking place.

'Three cars already,' said Stuart, with enthusiasm. 'You don't get that at the Falls of Lingarry. It's walking and climbing all the way there.'

'And you've got to mind how you go,' agreed Ailsa, 'and no running on ahead here either. It's fun going to the Falls, but it's dangerous, too.'

They set off along the narrow track, squelching through marshy ground, while Stuart picked his way, fleet of foot. Ailsa insisted that they pause now and again, while she looked round at the beauty of the mountains, with small silver lochs in the distance. There was a mist on one of the hills, however, and she shivered a little in her warm anorak, then took Stuart's hand again.

At the Falls she forgot everything else, however, as she looked at the grandeur of the wall of water which thundered over the rocks, the highest waterfall in Britain. She clung firmly to Stuart's hand when he ventured too close, and he turned to her pityingly.

'Are you a wee bit feart, Ailsa?' he asked, his voice kindly.

Another party of young climbers who were making their way back heard the remark and one of the girls caught Ailsa's eye, smiling.

'I am, rather,' she admitted. 'I think you'd better take me back again, Stuart.'

In an odd sort of way she had been 'feart', she thought, as they began to retrace their steps, finding it hard going at times. There had been something ominous about the Falls, which she had never experienced before, and she was glad when they could at last see her small car, parked with others, like small toys in the valley.

'Let's sit here and eat our sandwiches,' said Stuart, finding a grassy mound. 'Anice should have come, shouldn't she?'

'She should feel free to decide that for herself,' said Ailsa.

'She's no fun these days,' repeated Stuart. 'We used to play games and we tried to get Davina to play, but she wouldn't.'

'What sort of games?'

'Exciting ones. For a dare. Only Davina was a poor bit craitur.'

'Oh, Stuart!' said Ailsa, unsure whether or not to laugh. The quicker he was sent to school, and away from all his old-fashioned ways, the better.

'She learned to drive, though,' conceded Stuart. 'Anice told her that Iain would get fed up with her being so peelie-wallie.'

Ailsa's expression sharpened as she looked at the boy. She should have questioned Stuart more closely before, remembering past opportunities.

'She didn't really believe that, did she?'

'Och, we could make her believe anything, Anice and me. I tell you she was a poor bit craitur.'

'Stop saying that!' commanded Ailsa, abruptly. 'Stuart, you . . . you hadn't dared her to do anything when she went away?'

'Och no. It was no fun any more, and Anice started to get all grown up and to wear fancy skirts and things. Girls are all alike,' he said disgustedly, 'and Iain. Iain grew too busy after he got married. I wish you'd always stay with us, Ailsa,' he told her wistfully.

'You need boys of your own age to play with,' Ailsa told him, though she said it absently, her thoughts busy. For some reason she felt uneasy at what the child had told her, yet if she questioned Anice, she knew she would just get lies or evasive answers.

The girl was frightened, though she had put that down to fears about her mother's illness. Could it be that they had dared Davina to do something . . . some sort of challenge which she had accepted . . . from which she had not returned?

Cold fear began to take hold of Ailsa's heart, then common sense returned. If Davina had gone out on such an errand, someone must have found her. And why should she pack her clothes to do it?

At the same time, the two strong, stalwart and rather brash children could have made life very uncomfortable for their soft, gentle little sister-in-law, and Ailsa could well imagine Davina running away from that!

But what about Iain? Why should he allow such a thing to happen? Surely Davina, knowing that he loved her, would be able to laugh off the children's pranks.

'You're awful quiet, Ailsa.'

'I was just thinking,' she told him. 'Was Davina unhappy, Stuart?'

'I don't know,' he told her truthfully. 'She used to greet sometimes when Anice laughed at her, and Mother . . . my mother got mad at Anice. I used to go to Davey's house till Iain got home, and there was no arguing then.'

'I see,' said Ailsa.

She felt she was beginning to build up a picture of what Cardalloch was like as a home for Davina, and she did not like what she saw. Yet her cousin had not written to her, or given any hint that she was unhappy.

She drove the small Mini back along the rough track to the narrow main road, which skirted the loch, again, backing up to passing places when they met other cars head on.

Ailsa resolved to keep an eye on Anice. She was convinced now that the girl knew far more about Davina's whereabouts than she cared to admit.

9

Mrs McLaren did not respond very quickly to careful nursing, even though Anice looked after her devotedly, and Nurse McCall came to see her every day.

'Don't you think she'd be better in hospital?' Ailsa asked Dr Baird, and he stroked his chin, thoughtfully.

'Beds are hard to come by,' he said slowly, 'and even if she's slow to improve, it still is an improvement. There's nothing organically wrong with her. Maybe if you got her bed up to the window when it's fine, and got some fresh air into her . . .'

He was getting old, thought Ailsa uneasily, and resolved to have a word with Iain. Lena McLaren should not be so ill without more being done for her.

Still, Davina's dressing-room had tall

glass windows which opened out on to a small balcony. Perhaps Lena could be moved in there . . .

Ailsa went along to the dressing-room thoughtfully, and looked in. It wore an air of neglect, and she went forward to throw open the window, deciding that it could so with a good clean and polish, whether Lena wanted to use it temporarily or not.

She was tidying some shoes into a large cupboard, when she caught sight of something pushed to the back of the top shelf. It was probably something else which needed to be tidied, thought Ailsa, lifting over a chair and standing on it. A moment later she lifted down a blue leather suitcase.

Ailsa's eyes grew dark when she saw it, and she hurried to open it, her mouth going dry at the sight of the contents, recognising the distinctive dress, housecoat, underwear and other items of clothing which had been missing from Davina's wardrobe.

Ailsa sat down shakily, unable to sort

out the significance of her find for a moment or two, then she pulled herself together and walked briskly along to Lena's room, where Anice was sitting reading a book while her mother slept.

'Can you come along here for a moment, Anice?' Ailsa asked, as levelly as she could, and the girl set her book aside a trifle reluctantly, and followed Ailsa back along to Davina's dressing-room.

'I understood you to say Davina had taken her case with her, and you showed me that this blue and emerald dress was missing, also her housecoat. Yet here they are . . . in this suitcase. Can you explain this, Anice?'

The girl had gone chalk-white and backed towards the door, but Ailsa would not allow her to go so easily.

'What about it, Anice?'

'She . . . she must have h . . . hidden them away on top of the cupboard.'

'How did you know I found it on top of the cupboard?'

Anice looked sickly. 'I don't know,' she whispered.

'Because you put it there? Anice, I think you've got a lot of explaining to do. Where is Davina?'

Suddenly the girl's shoulders were heaving. 'I don't know.'

'I think you do. You've been trying to cover her tracks. Come on, Anice, where did she go?'

'I don't know!'

The girl's voice rose almost to a shout, then she turned, trembling, as Iain strode along the corridor, and looked in, his breath catching at the sight of the two girls with the suitcase between them.

Ailsa watched the colour drain from his face.

'Where did this come from?' he asked, almost in a whisper. 'It's . . . it's Davina's case. She . . . had it with her on our honeymoon. You said it was missing, Anice.'

'It was on the top shelf of this cupboard, hidden at the back,' said

204

Ailsa. 'I'm asking Anice what she knows about it . . . where Davina is.'

'She went out,' whispered Anice. 'She went out walking. For a dare.'

'And?'

'She . . . she didn't come back in again.'

'And you said nothing?' asked Iain, his eyes dark and glittering. 'You said nothing? Where did she go?'

The girl shook her head, sobs beginning to shake her body.

'Where?'

'To the Falls of Lingarry.'

There was heavy silence, then Iain rushed from the room, calling over his shoulder that he would deal with Anice later.

Ailsa sat down in bewilderment, all sorts of questions chasing themselves round in her mind. Davina would have to be practically browbeaten to go up the Falls unless for some good reason.

'It wasn't just for a dare, was it, Anice?' she asked quietly.

'It was a dare.'

'No, it wasn't. I know Davina, don't forget. She would never do such a thing just for a dare. She would have to be goaded into it. Why did she go?'

'I don't know, I tell you. For a dare.'

Anice turned and she, too, ran from the room. Ailsa could hear her heels clicking as she fled downstairs. She sat for a long time, hardly able to take in what was happening. Weeks ago her cousin had walked out one afternoon to tramp up to the Falls of Lingarry . . . and had not come home again. And Anice had packed her suitcase and hidden it, to pretend that Davina had gone off somewhere on her own.

A faint cry penetrated into her jumbled thoughts, and she hurried back along to Lena McLaren, who was pulling herself up on the pillows, her cheeks burning with colour.

'You left the doors open,' she said weakly. 'I heard.'

Ailsa bit her lip, blaming herself for such a mistake.

'Don't you worry about it. Iain's taking care of it.'

'No, I'm glad something like this has turned up. It was Anice, wasn't it? I thought there was something, but I didn't know. It's worse not to know, only to suspect.'

'Suspect what, Mrs McLaren?'

'She was jealous of Davina. I know she upset her, but I don't know how. Davina should not have bothered about her, but she let Anice get on top of her at every turn. It was my fault, too. I . . . I should have told Iain when I couldn't control Anice myself, only I was afraid he . . . he'd make us leave Cardalloch. I was to blame, too.'

Weak tears rolled down her cheeks, and Ailsa wiped them with her soft white handkerchief and tried to comfort her, even though she felt appalled by what she was hearing.

'It's all right,' the older woman told her, taking the handkerchief from Ailsa.

'I . . . I'll be better now. It was the worry which was pressing in on me. I . . . I didn't know, you see. I suspected something like this, but it could easily have been as . . . as Anice said every time I asked her, and I was glad to think it, to believe it.'

'Will you be all right while I go to see what Iain is doing?' asked Ailsa, rising.

'Oh aye,' the woman said wearily, 'I'll be all right now. I'll pull myself together and get up. Someone has to deal with Anice, and it had better be me. I . . . I know she's a child, at an awkward age, but I should have brought her up better. Perhaps . . . perhaps it would have been different if her own father had not died.'

Ailsa left her and walked downstairs where Ina Blair was rushing about packing coffee and sandwiches. Iain and Jim Blair were organising yet another search party. There was no sign at all of Anice, and Stuart, coming in from a visit to Davey's, looked rather white and frightened.

'Go up and see your mother, Stuart,' Ailsa commanded him quickly. 'I'll bring you both something to eat on a tray. Have you seen Anice?'

'Iain sent her to tell Alec McNair, to his cottage. He can't reach home on the phone. The polis is on his way, too.'

Ailsa ran off to find McLaren.

'Iain! Iain, she can't be there. You've searched there before, many times. If she had been there, she . . . she would have been found . . . '

He looked at her almost blindly.

'We will search again and again, till we find her,' he said woodenly, and she shivered as she turned away.

Anice returned after the search party had been gone for a quarter of an hour.

'Alec McNair wasn't in,' she said wearily. 'Probably he's up in the hills, at his hide.'

In spite of herself, Ailsa felt pity for the girl.

'I'll find him,' she said quickly. 'I

know where to go. You get some tea. I've just made some.'

'I don't want any.'

'Yes, you do.'

Anice was sobbing again. 'I never meant her to go,' she said thickly. 'I only told her . . . Iain was probably falling out of love with her since she was such a puny sort of wife. She was so easy to tease. When she said she — she'd leave her red hankie at the top of the Falls, and Iain could go and collect it, I thought she was joking. Then she didn't come back, and . . . and I was frightened, so I pretended she'd just . . . gone away . . . '

'But she could have been lying there injured!' cried Ailsa, her eyes full of horror.

'She wasn't! She wasn't! I went there myself to look. She was wearing her bright blue anorak and I'd have seen her, only there was no sign of her, and the men went there often. I even told the police she . . . she might have gone there, but the police didn't find her. I only . . . I only kept it from Iain and Mother and . . . and you . . . Iain would have been mad. He's mad now, isn't he?'

There was something touching in the girl's dark distressed eyes, and Ailsa guided her to a chair by the fire.

'You'll have to get some sweet tea,' she said briskly. 'It won't do if we have you ill as well.'

Ailsa did her best to see to Anice, even as her thoughts still churned round and round. There was still something missing. Davina was not such a fool as to do anything so stupid, and for such a reason. Anice must still be keeping something back. Yet she could not question the girl further. For the moment Anice had had quite enough.

It was shortly afterwards that Ailsa took her small car and drove up into the hills as far as she could go, then began to walk up to Alec's hide.

* * *

Alec was already coming down from the hide and making for his Range-Rover, when Ailsa caught sight of him as he carried several items of equipment.

He paused at the sight of her, then strode forward even as she hurried to meet him, everything else forgotten in the sudden desire to be with him again. For a moment he put down the haversack and other things he was carrying, and she went into his arms while he held her close, alarmed by her white face and trembling body.

'It's Davina,' she said at length. 'Davina.'

The journey to find him had thrown her into her own company, and her own thoughts, for the first time that day, and with solitude had come fear, and a realisation of what it could all mean.

'Take your time, my dear,' Alec told her, his hands on her shoulders.

'We . . . we've found her case, and . . . and Anice says she really went to the Falls of Lingarry. Iain . . . ' she paused again, and breathed deeply. 'Iain has organised another search party. Could . . . could you go, Alec? Iain . . . I think he needs you very badly.'

Her face was white with distress, and her eyes full of longing as she looked up at him, and just for a moment his face darkened as he looked down at her, his hands still gripping her shoulders so tightly that it hurt, yet she hardly noticed the pain.

'Jealousy can do terrible things to us, Ailsa,' he said, rather hoarsely.

'You . . . you mean you're jealous of Iain?'

'For my sins,' he said roughly, then hurried into action again, picking up his belongings. 'This is no time for personal feelings, though. I'll get up to the Falls right away. What about your aunt and uncle?'

Ailsa's heart sank. 'I'm going there now,' she said quickly. 'I . . . I'll have to explain to them.'

Alec's eyes softened as he looked down at her.

'They're courageous people,' he told her quietly, 'and they've got a very courageous niece.'

'What about Will Gregg?' she asked. 'Could he help?'

Alec considered. 'If we need him, I'll send for him.'

She watched him leave, then returned to her own small car. Alec would need all his courage, too, if he loved Davina. And he must love her, or why else should he be jealous of Iain? Yet the thought of her cousin drove everything else from her mind, as she drove over to Kilcraig, where the news had already been received, no doubt via Ina Blair and Bella.

★ ★ ★

Aunt Elizabeth rose, white-faced, to greet Ailsa when she walked in.

'We must try to hope, Auntie,' Ailsa told her, holding the older woman in her strong young arms. 'Shall I ask Uncle Robert to come home again?'

Elizabeth shook her head.

'Let's wait for news,' she said, in a low voice. 'Don't leave me, Ailsa.'

'I won't,' she was promised.

The hours seemed to pass endlessly, but at length the men came back home, and Iain and Alec McNair both walked over to Kilcraig.

'We've combed every inch of the ground,' said Iain wearily. 'There was no sign of her anywhere . . . only a red hankie wedged into some rocks near the top of the Falls.'

Ailsa caught her breath. 'Then she *has* been there!' she said excitedly, and told them about Anice's story of the dare. The hot blood rushed into Iain's cheeks.

'I shall see her when I get back,' he said tightly. 'If she's been tormenting my wife . . . '

'Then you should have known about it,' put in Alec, deceptively gentle.

'How can one always know what

women get up to?' asked Iain, his eyes glittering with anger.

'How can you not know?' countered Alec, and Ailsa saw an explosive situation brewing up between the two men.

'It's hardly the time to go over old ground,' she said sharply. 'You're both very tired. Perhaps motives could be examined later, but I think I ought to get Aunt Elizabeth to bed.'

Immediately they were both solicitous, though Alec's face was white and hard as granite. Of the two it was hard to tell which man was the more upset.

'Don't forget that Anice is very young,' she pleaded with Iain. 'I don't think she had any thought of mischief.'

Iain looked at her broodingly. 'I've made many mistakes,' he admitted. 'One of them was Anice . . .'

'And another Davina?' asked Alec, his blue eyes sparking dangerously as he looked at Iain, then back at Ailsa.

Iain faced him squarely. 'As I said,

I've made my mistakes,' he said quietly. 'I only ask for the chance to put a few right.'

'We would all like such a chance, McLaren. It happens to few of us.'

'Please,' whispered Ailsa. 'Please, Iain, Alec . . . there's no point in quarrelling.'

She looked after both of them as they went their separate ways, and her heart felt painful. They both loved Davina, and were obviously suffering a great deal by her disappearance, and she . . . she loved Alec McNair, and would never love anyone else.

'Ailsa,' said Aunt Elizabeth shakily, 'isn't it possible to be lost at the Falls and . . . and not to be found?'

'Ssh,' said Ailsa. 'Don't think of such a thing. Of course it couldn't happen!'

But it could, she thought, with a dry mouth. It was something which must be in the minds of all of them.

★ ★ ★

Hugh came two days later, a rather subdued Hugh, who no longer decried his sister's selfishness, nor insisted on having Ailsa in Edinburgh. He eyed his mother anxiously, and found an opportunity to talk to Ailsa alone. He looked troubled and anxious.

'We both know the Falls, Ailsa,' he said, after a long pause. 'What do you think?'

'I don't know,' she said wearily. 'We're all worried, Hugh, and trying not to show it.'

'Why on earth would Davina go there on her own, just to prove something?' he asked, though there was nothing but sadness in his voice.

Ailsa shook her head, though there was a spark of purpose in her eyes. Anice could tell her more, she thought, with determination. She had been sorry for the girl, realising how young and frightened she was, but now she was going to dig deeper, and Anice was going to help.

'I'm trying to find out all I can,'

she told Hugh. 'If . . . if mistakes have been made, then we must insure that they aren't made again.'

'I've got to get back to Edinburgh,' said Hugh, 'but I'll be back as soon as I can. Come and see me off.'

She went to the door with him after he had said goodbye to his mother, and for a moment he hesitated on the steps, then held Ailsa tightly, kissing her.

'I'm glad you're here,' he told her, and abruptly walked towards his car.

Ailsa bit her lip, seeing that Alec McNair had been coming down the drive, and was now hesitating. Then he turned and strode back through the gate.

He had seen Hugh kiss her, thought Ailsa, then remembered, rather dejectedly, that it did not really matter what he had seen.

★ ★ ★

'Why can't you leave me alone, Ailsa?' moaned Anice next day, when the older girl called in at Cardalloch and insisted on speaking to her. 'Mother's a lot better now, and we're both managing to run the house without your interference. It's like it always was, and always should be. We don't need you any more.'

There was new defiance in her look, and Ailsa acknowledged it levelly.

'I'm glad of that, Anice. Believe me, my time is more precious to me than to spend it on interference. I can't refuse help, though, if it's needed and I can give it.'

'Then what do you want? Iain's busy. He doesn't need you.'

'It's you I've come to see, Anice. You see, the only reason we have for Davina behaving foolishly and entirely out of character by going off and climbing up to Lingarry alone is the one you've given us. That she did it for a dare.'

'She did! She did!'

'And something else besides,' said Ailsa quickly. 'Davina just wouldn't have done something she hated for a dare, just to satisfy you and Stuart. It won't wash, Anice. I just don't believe it.'

'She was soft. Iain should never have married her. I told her . . . ' Anice broke off, biting her lip. 'We all knew it,' she said, more quietly. 'She was far too colourless to be mistress of Cardalloch.'

The girl threw back her head, and Ailsa caught her breath, again seeing the girl's astounding beauty, and the proud, almost fanatical light in her eyes.

'So what did you tell her, Anice?' she asked softly, 'that someone . . . someone else would have been a better choice?'

The girl gazed at her, and there was sudden knowledge between.

'Yes,' she said, her eyes glittering. 'Yes, that's what I told her. I told her Iain wasn't my brother and that I had belonged to him . . . always. She knew what I meant. She believed me.'

In spite of being prepared for something of the kind, Ailsa felt a sense of horror as she gazed at the girl, then she heard a startled exclamation behind her, and Iain walked slowly forward, having just come into the room.

'What? WHAT did you say?' he demanded, and Anice seemed to shrink again.

'N . . . nothing. I was only joking.'

'A childish joke?' he asked, his eyes blazing. 'Just what did you tell Davina?'

'The truth. That I'm no child,' she flung at him, 'as I keep telling you, Iain.' Suddenly she was pleading with him. 'Why didn't you wait, Iain? I'm not your sister, but you *must* know I love you properly. Not as a little sister . . . as a woman. See, Iain . . . ' She stood in front of him, holding herself almost like a ballet dancer and twirling round, her arms above her head, the light falling on the beauty of her face and long black hair. 'I'm a woman, Iain.'

'Stop it!'

He looked terrible in his anger, and again Ailsa saw Anice crumble and the childish tears rush to her eyes.

'It was only a joke, honestly. I mean, Davina would know it wasn't really true. She didn't believe it. It didn't make her rush off like that. It was something else . . . it must have been. I told her she would find Alec McNair up there. He's often around there, and she was always talking to him. She should have married Alec, not you, Iain.'

Swiftly his hand reached out and gripped her arm.

'Go to your mother,' he said, very quietly. 'I shall see you later, when I know what arrangements can be made for you.'

Her eyes were dark as she turned to Ailsa and the older girl shivered, trying to remember that Anice was so young, yet she could only see the woman in her. It was obvious that Davina, too, had only seen the woman. Had she made that climb in sheer bravado, trying to overcome her fears that Anice had told the truth about herself and Iain? Could Davina have believed her?

Iain was already asking her the same question as Anice left the room.

'She couldn't believe such a thing,' he said, almost to himself. 'Yet she changed so. She was so quiet and she used to look at me as though she had to make up her mind about something.'

'Didn't you ask her?' asked Ailsa.

Slowly he shook his head.

'It was like a barrier of glass. It built up so that we couldn't reach each other through the barrier. I . . . I thought she was beginning to lose her love for me, that she was disappointed in our married life. And Anice kept saying she had seen Davina talking to McNair. I . . . I suppose I grew jealous, hardly realising what was happening. She kept telling me things . . . showing off a little about how she was learning to drive, and how well she could ride . . . I thought she was bored!'

He came and took Ailsa's hands, holding them tightly.

'She won't come back . . . not ever, will she, Ailsa?'

Her own breath caught in her throat, and she tried to keep fear out of her eyes.

'Nobody has found her yet, Iain,' she pointed out quietly. 'I think . . . if she had fallen . . . she would have been seen. She was wearing bright clothes, remember? Don't give up hope, Iain.'

'Then where is she?'

'Trying to work Anice out of her system, perhaps,' she told him quietly. 'But I don't know where.'

'And you don't think she was gradually turning to McNair?'

'I'm quite sure she wasn't,' Ailsa said stoutly.

She was glad, though, that Iain had not asked if Alec loved Davina.

10

After Hugh went, Kilcraig settled down again rather uneasily. Bella Donaldson was inclined to fuss over Aunt Elizabeth, even more than usual, and Hector went around in his quiet purposeful fashion. Usually visitors to the area gave him a great deal of interest, and he enjoyed relating to Ailsa all about people staying at various cottages, or in caravans.

'One of the foresters has been here, wanting a word with you,' he informed Ailsa, after offering to give her small Mini a check-over.

'Who?' she asked.

'Will Gregg. His mother was here for a great many years . . . '

'Nanny Gregg!' cried Ailsa. 'Oh dear, I'd promised to go and see her, Hector, and it slipped my mind.' A thought struck her. 'She'll have heard about

Davina, I suppose, and she used to be her nanny. She'll . . . she'll be upset, Hector.'

'Aye, she will.' Hector spoke heavily. 'I think that's why Will has been here wanting you. He said he had been busy helping Mr McNair or he'd have come before.'

'Then Mr McNair is finished now? At the hide, I mean?'

'Och yes. I can't see there's much to interest him there. The birds come and go, and they nest and bring up their young. It's happening all the time, Miss Ailsa.'

She laughed. 'If the bird is rare, then it interests Mr McNair very much indeed, and people enjoy watching wild life which is being preserved.'

'What about when birds are preserved in some countries, then get shot down when they fly off somewhere else? What good is that?'

'Perhaps countries can get together over that problem, Hector,' she said mildly, knowing that he often argued for the sake of arguing.

Yet she knew, now, that Alec would be working at his cottage each day, no doubt writing up his notes and editing his film and tape. Yet he had not asked her to come over and help.

And now there was Nanny Gregg, who would want to know all that had been happening with regard to Davina.

'How do I get to the cottage, Hector? Nanny Gregg's cottage, I mean. Can I take the car?'

'Och, it's rough track and you'd be better walking, Miss Ailsa, though you'll need a rest when you get there. It was a shepherd's cottage up there among the hills, but Will prefers the forestry. His father was a rare one wi' the sheep. Now, if you take this road and turn off where it forks, and keep to your left . . .'

Hector gave detailed instructions, and Ailsa stopped him, then wrote it all down.

'Maybe Nanny Gregg would welcome

a few extra things,' she said. 'She must be a bit cut off.'

'She has the wireless,' Hector assured her. 'She listens to all the record programmes and women's programmes. She fair likes to hear that pop music.'

Ailsa's eyes gleamed with recollection. Nanny Gregg had always been gay and full of fun. She felt rather better, now, about going to see her. It was unlikely that Nanny Gregg would be the helpless old woman she had imagined.

The weather had been unsettled for a few days, which meant that every now and again the heavens opened and poured down torrential rain. The gutters became choked, and Aunt Elizabeth and Hector had words over the clearing of leaves from the gutters.

On the first fine day, Ailsa surveyed the settled weather with satisfaction and decided that she needed a good walk in the fresh air, and Nanny Gregg's would be just far enough.

'It's a good hour's tramp,' Hector

had informed her, scratching his head.

That meant an hour and a half at least, as far as Ailsa was concerned, and she set out carrying a few delicacies for Nanny Gregg and some sandwiches and chocolate for herself in case she felt hungry.

The narrow path wound round the sides of the hill, and Ailsa paused now and again to look down on Kilcraig which looked even more beautiful in its peaceful setting, viewed from above. She could see Cardalloch in the distance, and the river rushing angrily along the valley, in full spate after the heavy rain, its brown water frothing and churning.

In contrast the small springs which she passed from time to time tinkled merrily, and Ailsa paused to admire a gigantic spider's web, clearly reflected by sun and water. The sun also sparkled on the stones, making up the rough path, and she bent to pick up one or two small ones, admiring their smooth shape, and putting them in her pocket.

Inevitably her thoughts turned to Alec McNair, who had rung over for her when she had gone to Kyle in the car, leaving a message with Bella for her to ring back.

'Best ring now, Miss Ailsa,' Bella had told her when she walked in with her shopping basket. 'Mr McNair sounded urgent.'

'Thank you, Bella,' she said, her heart leaping.

There had been no reply, and later she had decided that there was no use in contacting Alec again. It was best to try to forget him, even if his bright blue eyes were constantly in her mind's eye, whether full of laughter or contempt.

Now she wished she had telephoned again. Maybe half a loaf was better than no bread.

Had Will Gregg run down this very road to school each day, years ago? she wondered, pausing for breath. She wouldn't have blamed him for playing truant now and again!

Finally she rounded a corner and

saw the small cottage perched on the hillside as though it had been painted on by an artist.

Yet it was very much alive, Ailsa could see, judging by the curl of white smoke from the chimney, and the snowy white sheets, pillowcases and towels blowing on the line.

There was no garden, and the cottage seemed to grow straight out of the hillside, though the pretty white curtains behind shining windows made it look cosy and protected. Ailsa saw a curtain move as she walked up to the door, which flew open before she could knock. Nanny Gregg stood there, looking old but strong and upright in her large white apron and her grey hair tied back in a bun. Her eyes, almost as blue as Alec's, surveyed her appraisingly.

'Hello, Nanny,' Ailsa greeted her. 'Your son Will left a message asking me to call.'

'You've been a long time about it, Miss Ailsa.'

Ailsa grinned, remembering that tone of old.

'But I only got the message a day or two ago, Nanny,' she protested mildly.

'Do you tell me that? Best come in, though. It's a sair climb when you're not used to it.'

Ailsa stepped inside the cottage which was a trifle dim after the bright sunshine. She was aware of another figure sitting by the fireside, and paused, blinking.

'Hello, Ailsa,' said Davina. 'So you've come at last.'

Shock rooted Ailsa to the floor, then she began to tremble as a mixture of emotions swept over her.

'Davina! Davina, what are you doing here?'

Her voice choked on the question, and she burst into tears.

'There, I told you she wouldn't know, Miss Davina. Come on, now, there's a good girl. Just you drink this.'

A large thick mug of hot tea, well sweetened, was pressed into her hand, and Ailsa drank it gratefully.

'Now, sit down,' said Nanny Gregg, pushing her into an old green plush chair. 'Get your breath back, Miss Ailsa, and I'll tell you how it all happened. Miss Davina is a lot better now, but not able for herself yet. She'd better just sit quietly and let me do the talking.'

Now that she could see more clearly, Ailsa's eyes were on her cousin. Davina was like a very delicate angel, sitting by the fireside in an ancient white cambric nightdress, heavily embroidered at neck and wrist. Her face was pale as milk and her fair hair hung in braids on her shoulders.

'She's had a sore arm and a sore knee,' Nanny was explaining. 'I've had to poultice them for her. It was where she fell, the silly lass.'

'Did you get the doctor?'

'Och, what would I be wanting wi' the doctor away up here? The old soul would be an invalid himself by the time he got this length. Anyway, she had nothing wrong with her that I couldn't put right . . . well, maybe one thing, but I doubt it would take more than the likes of me to put *that* right.'

She glared at Davina, who turned her head away.

'I should have skelped her oftener as a wee thing, but somebody should have skelped McLaren even harder! And as for that young lass, Anice . . . well! She's the one that needs the doctor!'

'Can't you start at the beginning?' asked Ailsa, her head beginning to swim. 'How did Davina come to be here?'

'Because Will carried her here. She'd gone climbing up to Lingarry, then when she was coming away, she slipped on a loose stone and fell. Only the good Lord kept her from falling in, and as it was, she had to cling to some rough heather before Will got hold of her. By then she was feeling the pain of her knee and arm, so he carried her here because it was nearer than Cardalloch.'

Ailsa's eyes began to blaze.

'But why on earth didn't you tell Mr McLaren and . . . and Aunt Elizabeth? They were nearly out of their minds!'

For the first time Nanny looked sheepish.

'I know,' she said, with a sigh. 'We should have done, Will and me, in spite of all her pleading . . .'

'No,' broke in Davina. 'No, Nanny! I told you . . . no!'

Nanny Gregg looked at Ailsa. 'You see, Miss Ailsa?'

'I see. But, Davina, you can have no notion what it was like, not knowing where you had gone. We thought *all* sorts of things. At first we thought you had just gone away, because . . . oh well, never mind that now . . . but later we thought you had fallen in over the Falls, and men have given hours of their time to look for you. At one time we even wondered if you'd run away with . . . with Alec McNair, and he was embarrassed by suspicion.'

For the first time a smile of amusement lit up Davina's face.

'Poor Alec! I expect, though, that he had plenty to say if he got the blame for that.'

'He did,' Ailsa assured her.

'I put her to bed, and she took very bad,' said Nanny Gregg, 'and kept asking us just to keep her quiet. She didn't want to go back till she was able, and she thought they'd make her go back if they knew her whereabouts.'

'They?'

'McLaren, and her mother and father, I suppose. I knew there was some trouble between her and McLaren, so I heeded her, and just nursed her here till she felt better.'

'But didn't you realise what a terrible thing it was? Having us all believe the worst? Her husband has been frantic with worry.'

'He'll be glad to be rid of me,' said Davina tonelessly, 'and if I'd gone to

Mother and Daddy, they would just have made me go back to Iain. And . . . and I couldn't face it . . . Iain not loving me . . . loving An . . . Anice instead.'

Davina's voice had begun to choke.

'He doesn't! He doesn't!' cried Ailsa. 'He never loved Anice . . . '

'That makes it worse,' whispered Davina. 'I know what they were . . . to each other.'

'It wasn't true,' said Ailsa desperately.

'It was.' Davina's voice was toneless but steady. 'I saw.'

'You . . . you?'

'I saw them myself, with my own eyes. I saw.'

Ailsa felt as though she had received a body blow.

'So I thought if he wanted a flamboyant, strident devil-may-care sort of woman, he could have one. I told Anice I'd accept her challenge and go up Lingarry on my own, and leave her red hankie there.'

'Hers?'

'Yes, hers. Perhaps it was stupid. I . . . I don't know. I couldn't think straight and she was laughing and . . . and wearing my best skirt and blouse, too. She said Iain had only married me because he needed money, and I was to ask him and see. Only he'd gone, and I couldn't ask him anyway. There was only Anice there, laughing and laughing . . . '

'There then,' soothed Nanny Gregg. 'She was distraught, Miss Ailsa, and no wonder. Fine goings on, I must say, yet I wouldn't have thought it of McLaren, and the mistress so set on him, too. That's why I kept Miss Davina quiet here, till I saw how the land lay. Will kept his eye on things, though he'd have told when they started looking at the Falls, if he'd been there at the time. He didn't find out till later, since he was helping Mr Alec. Only if we'd brought her back at the time, Miss Ailsa, she . . . she might have had her brain in a fever.' Nanny's eyes were pleading. 'She's just beginning to come to herself now, so we thought it was best to bring you up. Will went to find you at Kilcraig, only you were out, then he asked Mr Alec to tell you to come up, and Hector Donaldson before that. We left plenty of messages.'

'Hector told me, but I didn't get any message from Alec,' said Ailsa, then remembered about the phone call. Had Alec just remembered the message?

'But Hector told me where to come, and I've just been waiting for a suitable day. Oh, Davina!' Suddenly the tears were flowing again, healing tears this time. 'Oh, Davina, I'm so glad you're safe,' she said, rather thickly, 'but I'm sure there must be some mistake about Iain. I'm certain that he loves you.'

'I loved him so,' said Davina dully, 'but Anice bewitched him. I shan't ever go back to him, Ailsa. I saw them, you see. I saw.'

Ailsa couldn't doubt the truth in her voice, and she felt sick and confused. Iain obviously had felt anger, no doubt tempered with affection, against Anice.

Ailsa had seen the rage on his face when he dealt with her. Yet could it have been rage caused by guilt and shame? He had told her he did not know why Davina had changed towards him.

'What did you see?' she asked, after a moment's thought.

'They were in each other's arms . . . in his study . . . they were kissing . . . '

Ailsa shivered at the harsh note in the young voice. No, Davina couldn't have imagined that.

'He'll have to know that . . . that you're here,' she said, at length.

'No!' Davina's voice was sharp, then she was again choking with sobs. 'No, Ailsa.'

'But they'll *have* to know . . . Iain, Aunt Elizabeth, Uncle Robert, Hugh . . . Alec . . . ' Her own voice trembled on the last name.

'Tell Alec,' Davina said quickly. 'You can tell Alec.'

'But the rest. You don't know what

241

it's been like, Davina.'

'Don't I?'

Nanny Gregg was shaking her head behind the girl's chair, and Ailsa took the hint and said nothing more.

'I'll have to go,' she said, after a while. Davina nodded. 'I'll come back, though. Will that be all right?'

She nodded again. 'Don't tell Iain. Don't tell anyone . . . except Alec . . . till I see what I want to do.'

Ailsa said nothing, unwilling to make any promises.

'We'll have to humour her,' said Nanny Gregg at the door. 'You can see she's still sick, Miss Ailsa.'

'I can see. But I've made no promises, Nanny Gregg. I shall have to think about it a bit longer.'

'And I'm thinking about my lass,' said Nanny firmly. 'She comes first wi' me. If they'd handled her right, she wouldn't be here.'

Ailsa bit her lip, wondering how true that was. She strode back down the hill road, hardly noticing the rough track, or the beauty of the distant purple mountains against a vivid blue sky.

'You can tell Alec,' Davina had said.

Yes, she could tell Alec. But what would happen then?

Ailsa went straight to Alec's cottage before going on to Kilcraig, feeling that she had to talk to someone before she saw Aunt Elizabeth and Uncle Robert again . . . or even Iain.

Alec opened the door himself, gazing at her, then gently guiding her inside when he saw her obvious distress.

'Ailsa, my dear! What's happened? It . . . it isn't . . . Davina?'

She nodded. 'But not the way you obviously think, Alec. She's all right. I . . . I know where she is.'

She saw the enormous relief in his eyes as he guided her into a chair.

'Take your time, then, Ailsa. You're all upset.'

She nodded again, feeling the comfort of his arm about her shoulder, then she began to tell him Davina's story, watching his face begin to harden when she explained about Anice and Iain.

'How could he!' cried Alec furiously. 'How could he do such a thing to her?'

'I don't think he did,' said Ailsa, shaking her head. 'I think there's a mistake somewhere. Iain would never hurt Davina like that, or . . . or allow Anice to hurt her in any way. I'm sure of it.'

The glitter was back in Alec's eyes.

'Even now,' he said heavily, 'no matter what has happened, you'll fly to McLaren's defence. You can't believe he'd put a foot down wrong, can you?'

'No,' she said, stung, 'because it's true, and if you weren't so . . . so jealous of him, you'd see he's not that sort of person. He would never encourage another woman under his wife's roof.'

'All right, so I am jealous of him. I admit it,' flashed Alec, 'and I'm ashamed of it. But have you asked yourself why Davina would go to such lengths, if it weren't so? Have you asked yourself that?'

'She could be wrong,' Ailsa persisted. 'Maybe you can be equally blind over Davina that you can't see how imaginative she can be.'

'Imagine? Imagine all that? Wake up, Ailsa.'

Suddenly her anger began to go, leaving her cold and shivery. She had hoped she could talk it all over sensibly with Alec, and she could then see clearly what was to be done, but his jealousy, no doubt caused by his love for Davina, was clouding his judgement.

Ailsa's heart felt sore as she looked at Alec's tall broad figure as he walked up and down, then went to knock out his pipe and fill it from his tobacco jar. Why was it that of all men she should love this one, who didn't see her because his heart was filled by another woman?

And what of her own motives?

wondered Ailsa. Was she bent on pushing Davina and Iain together again, just to make sure Davina would never have Alec? Her cheeks coloured scarlet at the thought, and she told herself she had no such ideas. She was only concerned to see Davina happy again, and, remembering Iain's unhappy face, she was sure his happiness also lay with his wife.

'They love each other,' she said, half aloud. 'I'm sure of it.'

Alec's blue eyes scrutinised her again. 'So you've made up your mind?'

'They'll have to know,' she said defiantly. 'I can't keep them in ignorance.'

Alec sighed heavily. 'If you want my advice, then you'll see she isn't returned to the fold to endure the same circumstances all over again.'

'I think she just had a distorted view of things,' Ailsa said stubbornly.

She began to rise, and he reached towards her and pulled her into his arms, holding her so fiercely she could scarcely breathe.

'A man can get lonely for his woman, Ailsa,' he told her. 'Didn't you know that?'

'What happens if he hasn't got the right woman?' she asked, and he released her.

'He should make sure he *has* the right woman.'

'I agree,' she said, as calmly as she could, though her heart was thudding madly. 'I may be doing the wrong thing, but to do nothing is worse.'

'I hope you're right,' Alec told her. 'I hope so much that you are right.'

★ ★ ★

It was growing late, but Ailsa thought that it would still be early enough to see Iain, which was nearer Alec's cottage than Kilcraig.

'I'll come with you,' he said, reaching for his coat.

'No!' Her voice was sharp. 'This . . . this is something I have to do myself.'

He looked at her, then nodded agreement.

'Very well, if that's how you want it. Good luck, Ailsa . . . my dear!'

She felt a sob catching her throat at the sudden gentleness in his voice, and this time she wanted to stay and comfort him. He was big and strong, and looked as though he could take anything in his stride, but she could sense that he was also vulnerable, and could so easily be hurt.

But it was late by the time she reached Cardalloch, and Ailsa paused, feeling too tired to do more that evening, so she turned and walked home to Kilcraig.

Bella was looking for her, telling her that her aunt and uncle had gone to bed early.

'They didn't realise where you were, Miss Ailsa,' Bella told her reproachfully, 'so they didn't worry in case you'd got lost, as I did. Another five minutes and Hector would have been away looking for you.'

'I'm sorry, Bella. I . . . I rather forgot the time,' she said truthfully.

'Och well, I've a hot drink all ready for you.'

Ailsa paused, then nodded.

'I'll be glad of it, Bella. I'm tired.'

'That cottage is far too outlandish,' Bella said crossly. 'I used to tell Mrs Gregg that. She'd be far better down in the village.'

Ailsa didn't know whether or not she agreed with her.

11

Next morning Ailsa found that her aunt and uncle were planning to go into Plockton to attend to some business before her uncle returned to Edinburgh, and she sighed with relief. She felt she had to see Iain first, yet she could not have held normal conversation with either of them, knowing what she did, but unable to discuss it with them.

As soon as she could get away, she walked over to Cardalloch, where Ina Blair opened the door and informed her that Mrs McLaren was in the drawing-room.

'I've come to see Mr McLaren,' she said crisply.

'He's going out in a moment, Miss Ailsa.'

'I've still got to see him, Ina. Is he in the study?'

A moment later she was knocking

lightly on the study door. Iain wore a short coat over a thick jersey and tweed trousers. He looked up, surprised, when Ailsa walked in.

'Hello, Ailsa. An early visit . . . '

'I'm sorry, Iain. I had to come. I . . . I've got some news for you.'

'News?'

Immediately there was a stiffening in his face, and he stood up, facing her squarely. 'What news?'

'Can't we sit down for a moment? There's rather a lot to tell you.'

Again there was a pause, then he nodded briefly.

'I've found Davina, Iain,' she said simply.

The colour left his face completely. 'Where . . . where is she?'

'Up with Nanny Gregg, at the shepherd's cottage up beyond Lingarry.'

A moment later he had leapt to his feet, but she was before him, her back to the door.

'No, Iain. There's more to it than that!' she said sharply. 'She's ill . . . her nerves are very bad. She . . . doesn't want you to know.' As he showed signs of hardly hearing her, she repeated this loudly. 'She doesn't want you to know, Iain.'

He stopped, his eyes burning into hers.

'Why not?'

'She thinks you were having an affair with Anice.'

This time the blood mounted his cheeks till they were crimson.

'She must be . . . must be out of her mind,' he said, almost with disbelief. 'Why should she think such a thing? Anice is my sister!'

'No, she's not, Iain. She's a young lady, as she's shown you many times, and as you know yourself. She told Davina that very thing, or had you forgotten?'

He had. She could see it in his face, that in the heat of knowing where Davina was and the relief of knowing that she was safe, he had forgotten all about why she went away.

'Surely you told her!'

'I tried. But she's convinced of it. She *saw* you, Iain, you and Anice.'

'*Saw* us?'

This time there was nothing but bewilderment on his face. 'Saw us? What do you mean?'

'She says she saw you kissing Anice. The girl was wearing Davina's red skirt and new blouse at the time, if that's any guide.'

Slowly Iain sat down, running a hand through his hair as he tried to remember.

'Yes,' he said eventually, 'I'm remembering. Anice came to show me the clothes she said Davina had given her, and to ask if they didn't make her seem grown up. I said she looked very pretty, though I wasn't paying much attention. She's at a difficult age and sometimes makes a nuisance of herself. Then she threw her arms round my neck . . . '

Here Iain's face grew thunderous again.

'She kissed me, and I told her I wouldn't have such behaviour, and if she was growing up as she claimed, then she would only be treated as a young lady when she behaved like one. If . . . if Davina saw us, then she must have heard me . . . she *must* have . . .'

'She didn't. She only saw Anice in your arms.'

'Anice putting her arms round me,' corrected Iain. 'I thought she was teasing as she sometimes did. She needs something to do and she's going to Glasgow to train as a milliner. I'm taking a flat for her and her mother . . . they'll be happier there. Anice may meet some nice young man of her own age and fall in love properly, but if she doesn't settle . . . then, I suppose, I'll have to seek expert advice. Stuart is also going away . . . to school.'

He was talking mainly to clear his thoughts, then suddenly he was on his feet again.

'Come on, Ailsa. We're going up to the cottage.'

'But, Iain, don't you think . . . ?'

'No, I don't. She's my wife, Ailsa. I'm going to bring her home. We'll go in the Land-Rover. It can negotiate that road quite well.'

Ailsa's face was as white and strained as Iain's when they got out into his Land-Rover, and he began to drive with more speed than usual. It was as though some sort of desperate urgency was driving him on, but Ailsa's eyes were wide and dark as she wondered what sort of effect it would have on her cousin.

Iain gave Nanny Gregg little time to protest when the Land-Rover pulled up near the cottage, and somehow they were all inside, while Davina sat by the fire again, wearing her soft white nightdress, her fair hair in silken strands on either side of her small white face.

'Iain!' she whispered.

With a small cry the big man

lumbered forward and picked her up in his arms, holding her against his chest.

'My little darling,' he cried. 'Why did you do such a thing? I thought I'd lost you . . . for always. You must know I love you, and that Anice is only a child playing games.'

Ailsa retreated into the shadows while Nanny Gregg, soft tears on her cheeks, brewed up some of her strong tea, and offered them a cup. Ailsa could hear her cousin's trembling voice and Iain's deeper one resolving their misunderstandings.

'Obviously it's my fault if you ran away,' he told her. 'I wasn't looking after you properly. I . . . I thought you felt you'd made a mistake and wanted McNair.'

'Alec? Goodness, no!' Poor Alec, thought Ailsa, wincing. 'I was very silly, but I was so jealous,' said Davina. 'It's awful to be jealous, Iain.'

Ailsa bit her lip again. She wandered to the door, wondering if she could somehow go down and warn Aunt Elizabeth and Uncle Robert before Davina was brought home. Perhaps she ought to have told them after all . . .

'Ailsa!' She turned back into the cottage. 'We must get her home,' Iain was saying briskly, and Ailsa looked at him, amazed to see that he had shed several years, while happiness shone from both him and Davina.

'She's not fit yet,' Nanny Gregg was protesting.

'She could go to Kilcraig,' Iain said thoughtfully, 'and maybe Nanny Gregg could come, too, till Davina feels better. Then she can come home.'

He said this proudly, and Ailsa felt a lump catching her throat. Now there would only be the two of them, and Cardalloch would, indeed, be home.

'She'd be fair shook up in that contraption,' Nanny Gregg was still protesting.

'What about McNair's Range-Rover? That would be better. What do you think, Ailsa? Maybe you could take the Land-Rover down, and ask him, and see if the arrangements would suit Davina's mother and father at Kilcraig.'

Ailsa said nothing for a moment. Not long ago Iain and Alec were at each other's throats, but now, as far as Iain was concerned, it seemed to be all forgotten.

But what about Alec? He still held Iain responsible, and he loved Davina. How would he feel . . . ?

But he loved Davina, Ailsa thought again. He would not object to being of service to her. He would welcome that.

'Very well, I'll ask Alec,' she said. 'I'll go and attend to it all.'

She looked into her cousin's glowing face, and thought how young Davina looked.

'Oh, Ailsa,' she said, 'I'm so happy.'

'I'm glad, darling,' Ailsa said huskily, and went out quickly.

* * *

Alec said nothing for a moment when Ailsa called in with Iain's request.

'They've . . . they've ironed out all their misunderstandings,' she said, keeping her voice deliberately matter-of-fact. 'It was just misunderstanding, you know, Alec.'

He nodded slowly, but made no comment.

'So Iain wondered if you could do this for . . . for Davina . . . for both of them.'

'But of course,' said Iain readily. 'Ailsa, I . . . '

But she was looking away, because the tears were beginning to flood her eyes, and she had no wish to allow him to see her cry.

'I must go and tell Aunt Elizabeth and Uncle Robert. They don't know yet. They'll be so relieved . . . I must go, Alec.'

'Very well,' he told her. 'I'll deliver Davina to you safely. I'll be as quick as I can.'

'Thank you,' she said gratefully.

★ ★ ★

Aunt Elizabeth's reaction to the news that Davina was safe was the most emotional of all, and it was only then that Ailsa fully realised just what a strain it had been for her aunt.

'Oh, thank God, thank God,' she whispered tearfully, while Uncle Robert held her hand tightly, and couldn't trust himself to speak.

It was later, when the initial shock had worn off, and Davina's room all prepared for her arrival, that her aunt began to feel annoyed that there had been any need at all for the weeks of worry now behind her.

'Had she no thought for us at all, Ailsa?' she asked, the tears now flowing freely. 'Couldn't she have sent a note even, to set our minds at rest?'

'She was afraid,' Ailsa said simply. 'She thought you'd have made her go back to Cardalloch, and she was full of misunderstanding about the place.'

'Because of Anice?'

'Because of Anice.'

'The girl needs spanking. I hope Iain has had the good sense to deal with her properly.'

'She's to be trained for a proper job,' Ailsa said quietly. 'That seems to me the best way to deal with her. She met far too few people of her own age, and that wasn't good for a girl of her nature. When Davina is better, she will have to be mistress of Cardalloch without Lena's help.'

'That's how it should be,' said Aunt Elizabeth firmly. 'She won't have time, then, for silly ideas.'

Nevertheless, when the Range-Rover eventually arrived, bringing Davina with Iain and Nanny Gregg, Aunt Elizabeth forgot everything but the sight of her daughter again, and they all stood back a little while Davina was welcomed home by her parents. Ailsa rejoiced at the new happiness on Iain's face, her eyes resting on him softly.

Then she saw Alec slipping away quietly and ran after him to thank him.

'My pleasure,' he told her briefly. 'Believe me, I'm happy to see the girl home again.'

'Alec, I . . . I'm sorry if you've been hurt in any way,' she told him huskily, and he turned, the vivid blue eyes staring into hers.

'So am I,' he told her bluntly, then reached out to put strong hands on her shoulders. 'I suppose you won't consider marriage? Marrying me, I mean, Ailsa?'

Her heart leapt, then raced madly, and for a wild moment it would have been so easy to say yes. Then she remembered why she was being asked. Alec could see, now, that Davina belonged to Iain, and no doubt felt as lonely as she did herself.

Yet a loveless marriage was no solution, she thought dejectedly. Soon she would want more, much more, than he could give.

Slowly she shook her head, and his hands fell to his sides.

'All right,' he told her roughly, 'but

what a waste, Ailsa! They're married, for pity's sake. You can't undo that.'

She could hear his voice trembling with suppressed anger and felt pity and love for him sweep over her.

'I know,' she whispered. 'I'm sorry.'

A moment later he had gone.

★ ★ ★

Ailsa stayed on for a week to see Davina settled in, but soon it was obvious that she was no longer needed at Kilcraig. Soon Davina would be strong enough to go home to Cardalloch, and Nanny Gregg was going with her.

'It will be wonderful with just Iain and me,' she told Ailsa happily.

'You should have arranged it like that before,' the other girl said, and looked curious, remembering. 'Why didn't you? Iain gave you the chance.'

'I thought he wanted Anice there . . . I was a fool, wasn't I?'

'Yes, you were,' said Ailsa. 'Anyway,

you should be all right with just Nanny Gregg.'

The old nurse was very energetic for her age, and had often become bored at the isolated cottage, especially when the radio programmes were not to her liking. At Cardalloch she could even have television, something she greatly appreciated.

Aunt Elizabeth and Uncle Robert had decided to take a late holiday, since the trip to Canada had not gone according to plan, and Ailsa knew she would soon have to leave for Edinburgh.

She had seen very little more of Alec, though he walked over now and again to talk to Davina, bringing her an occasional fresh sea trout, which she loved.

'Alec's going to London next week,' she informed Ailsa. 'He's preparing a script for another Wild Life programme.'

'Oh,' said Ailsa.

'He's been showing me part of it,' went on Davina, giving Ailsa a sideways glance. 'He knows how interested I've always been in his nature programmes.'

Ailsa bit her lip, but said nothing as she carried on doing some mending for her aunt. They were leaving everything as shipshape as possible, with Bella and Hector to see to it.

'Only he needs it back tonight,' went on Davina, producing the script. 'I said Hector would bring it over, but he's away to Inverness with John McLean. Couldn't you take it over, Ailsa?'

'I . . . I'm packing,' Ailsa protested, rather hurriedly.

She felt she didn't want to see Alec again before she left. Surely the painful empty feeling she carried round inside her, would lessen in time, though seeing Alec was not the best way of trying to forget him.

'You've got heaps of time for that,' said Davina, surprised. She hesitated for a moment. 'Maybe . . . I suppose I *could* ask Iain . . . '

Ailsa bit her lip. It couldn't be any

easier for Alec seeing Iain again either, since he, too, was trying to fight against his love for Davina.

'I'll take it,' she said quickly.

'That's good,' beamed Davina. 'Thank you, Ailsa darling.'

★ ★ ★

That evening she walked over to the cottage, feeling that it could easily be for the last time. She would have no wish to come back to Kilcraig while Alec was so near, and her heart felt sore as she realised how much she loved the place, in spite of the midges which followed her in a cloud. She paused to reach into her bag for her tin of repellant, then marched forward again, with determination.

Alec had been fishing, and his rods and nets stood outside the door beside his waders. The appetizing smell of cooking sea trout wafted out to her at the door, and she pushed it open, calling for him.

He walked out of his large comfortable kitchen at the back of the house, his feet encased in thick dark green long woollen socks.

'Ailsa,' he said quietly, and she forced a smile.

'That smells good, Alec.'

Somehow the remark broke the tension between them and he pulled up another chair to the kitchen table and put out another knife and fork.

'There's enough to feed the five thousand,' he told her. 'The fishing was good at the head of the loch.'

'I'll enjoy this,' Ailsa told him frankly. 'It will be something to remember . . . when . . . when I go back.'

'When will that be?' he asked casually.

'Tomorrow. I'm going to Edinburgh.'

Alec said nothing, busying himself with serving up the rich pink fish.

'So you're going to Hugh,' he said, at length.

'Only to work for him.'

He sat down opposite to her.

'Then . . . then Iain has won after all, even if it can't mean anything to him. You would throw all the warmth and sweetness that is Ailsa into coffers which are already overflowing.'

She stared at him. 'I don't know what you mean. Or at least, I think I know, but you're quite wrong, Alec. I admire Iain as much as any man I know, but I've never really loved him, though I admit that I thought he was very attractive. But it wasn't love as I love . . . ' she hesitated, biting her lip, 'as *you* love Davina.'

'Davina? Yes, I suppose I do love Davina,' he said slowly, 'but only as a dear friend.'

Suddenly he was looking at her intently.

'Have we been at cross-purposes, Ailsa? It seems incredible . . . your eyes used to glow when you spoke of him and it seemed as though you loved him. Have we both been wrong?'

She hardly knew what to say, her

eyes drawn to his, seeing them gleam like sapphires.

'I don't know.'

'Surely I told you I loved you, and only you?'

She shook her head, and now he was rising and pulling her into his arms.

'Some men make poor lovers, Ailsa. They're afraid of having their love scorned. They're cowards. They're brave at going to war and fighting other men, but a woman can give them the greatest hurt of all. I know. I'm just such a coward, Ailsa, and you have it in your power to wound me or . . . or give me the greatest happiness I've ever known. Which is it to be, my love?'

She slipped into his arms, and he stroked her rich chestnut hair.

'I . . . I thought it was Davina, and I was so miserable, Alec, because I do love you so.'

'And I was jealous of poor old McLaren! Can you marry a fool, my Ailsa?'

'I can only marry you, Alec.'

The sea trout on sizzling hot plates began to grow cold, and outside the sun set in a glowing red sky.

* * *

Over at Kilcraig Aunt Elizabeth looked at the time and remarked, uneasily, that Ailsa was late in getting home.

'I shouldn't worry,' Davina told her mischievously. 'I lay you any odds you like she's getting engaged to Alec McNair. We'll be having another wedding in the family soon, Mother, you'll see.'

'Nonsense,' said her mother, then paused. 'Do you really think so, Davina?'

'I really think so,' she grinned. 'How much do you bet?' But, luckily for her, Elizabeth Campbell-Dene was not a betting woman.

We do hope that you have enjoyed reading this large print book.

Did you know that all of our titles are available for purchase?

We publish a wide range of high quality large print books including:
Romances, Mysteries, Classics
General Fiction
Non Fiction and Westerns

Special interest titles available in large print are:
The Little Oxford Dictionary
Music Book, Song Book
Hymn Book, Service Book

Also available from us courtesy of Oxford University Press:
Young Readers' Dictionary
(large print edition)
Young Readers' Thesaurus
(large print edition)

For further information or a free brochure, please contact us at:
Ulverscroft Large Print Books Ltd.,
The Green, Bradgate Road, Anstey,
Leicester, LE7 7FU, England.
Tel: (00 44) **0116 236 4325**
Fax: (00 44) **0116 234 0205**

Other titles in the
Linford Romance Library:

TO LOVE IN VAIN

Shirley Allen

When her father dies in a duel, Anna has no money to pay off his debts and is thrown into Newgate Gaol. However, she is freed by her cousin Julien, who takes her to her grandparents in France. Finding herself surrounded by people she cannot trust, Anna turns more and more to the handsome, caring Patrick St. Clair. Then, to her horror, she discovers her guardians are planning her marriage to a man of their choosing!

SHELTER FROM THE STORM

Christina Green

Kim takes a job on Dartmoor, trying to hide from her unhappy past. Temporarily parted from her son, Roger, and among unfriendly country neighbours, Kim finds the loneliness of the moor threatening, especially when her new boss's girlfiend, Fiona, seems to recognize her. Again, Kim runs. But Neil, her employer, soon finds her. When Kim discovers that he, too, has a shadow in his past, she stays on at Badlake House, comes to terms with life, and finds happiness.

A SUMMER FOLLY

Peggy Loosemore Jones

Philippa Southcott was a very ambitious musician. When she gave a recital on her harp in the village church she met tall, dark-haired Alex Penfold, who had recently inherited the local Manor House, and couldn't get him out of her mind. Philippa didn't want anything or anyone to interfere with her career, least of all a man as disturbing as Alex, but keeping him at a distance turned out to be no easy matter!